Look for More Titles by Cassandra Chandler

BRON

The Blades of Janus
PACK
PROGENITOR

The Forbidden Knights
FORBIDDEN INSTINCT

The Summer Park Psychics
WANDERING SOUL
WHISPERING HEARTS
LINGERING TOUCH

THE SUMMER PARK PSYCHICS OMNIBUS

Other Works
CRAFTING A WRITER'S LIFE: Building a Foundation

Coming Soon

Court of the Springtime Fae
Jack Frost
Prince Charming
The Oak King

Cygnian 7
TARN
ROM

Bron: A Scifi Alien Warriors Romance

Cygnian 7
Book Five

Cassandra Chandler

Copyright Page

This book is pure fiction. All characters, places, names, and events are products of the author's imagination or used solely in a fictitious manner. Any resemblance to any people, places, things, or events that have ever existed or will ever exist is entirely coincidental.

Bron: A Scifi Alien Warriors Romance
Cygnian 7, Book Five
Copyright © 2023 by Cassandra Chandler
Print ISBN: 978-1-945702-95-2
Digital ISBN: 978-1-945702-94-5

First eBook edition: December 2023
First print edition: December 2023
10 9 8 7 6 5 4 3 2 1

cassandra-chandler.com
P.O. Box 91
Mission, Kansas 66201

Prologue

Dean charged into his command center, clenching his fists tight enough that his nails dug deep grooves into his palms. His chest was heaving, even though he didn't actually need air to breathe. He had evolved beyond that sessions ago. Excruciating sessions in the growth chamber that was now destroyed, along with his second home on the *Reckoning*.

He should take *Outreach* from the infuriating Sadirians who had let this happen. Destroy their station and leave them scrambling, trapped in their ships as their only berth. Alone in the endless expanse of space. Alone, just as he was.

An image of Queenie flooded his mind, the kitten sitting back on her haunches and with her paws clasped before her, pleading for him not to destroy her home. He knew the pain of losing every sense of safety. Betrayal was an intimate acquaintance. He couldn't hurt her that way.

How could he have let himself grow to care so much for the little kitten?

Love was a weakness for enemies to exploit. It brought

only pain and failure. Dean should have listened to the lessons of his youth. His brother's actions were a greater teacher than his words. How many times was Dean going to let himself care about someone only to be abandoned again?

His brother. His partner, Serac. Now Queenie. No one stayed. No one.

Could he blame the kitten for wanting more than he could give? A home, a family? Some sense of permanence? What did he have to offer anyone?

The heart he had formed in this body pounded, responding to chemical signals replicated with absolute perfection. The chemicals that flooded him made his skin tingle and his muscles ache to do something. He wanted to swipe his arm across a table and knock everything to the floor, but he had locked down or sealed away everything on his ship. Having loose items on space ships was dangerous. Unfortunately, that meant there was nothing for him to use to vent his rage.

He couldn't blame the kitten. And he couldn't hurt her. This was his own fault, his own weakness. Dean should never have let himself care for another being. It was too late to change how he felt, and he wouldn't do anything to risk losing Queenie.

Especially not after he'd already lost Hayley.

The pain of her absence pulsed through him, twisting his guts and tightening the muscles beneath his skin. Dean lifted his hands to his head, grabbing his hair and pulling as he let out a scream. His skin rippled silver as his control over his shapeshifting slipped. The rage and despair were too much to contain, the pressure building till he thought he might explode. He let his shape morph with the emotion, arms turning silver and extending into sharp rods. Over and over, he struck the walls of his ship. The metal dented under his onslaught, his furious energy pouring into the relentless attack.

The computer sounded an alert—probably warning him of structural limits. He turned toward it, ready to crush the main control panel. Dean didn't even care anymore. Instead of the room being depicted on the main monitor with alerts about the damage he was doing, a humanoid figure filled the screen. A Cygnian. The one called Bron.

Dean paused, panting, his silvery arms hanging from his sides. They shortened, regaining their human appearance as he walked toward the monitor, reading the display. The computer had highlighted several areas of the Cygnian's body, pointing out his biomechanical alterations. The readings held more data than Dean had found during his own extensive investigation. *Much* more.

The scanner trap in Dean's lockbox was active. It had somehow pierced Bron's mechanical exterior and gathered information on his internal construction. The scanner identified Dean by his DNA and only allowed him access to the contents. In this case, with nothing biological to compare with, it had instead implanted several types of nanites and sent data to Dean—as it was programmed to do. Nanites that were now requesting instructions.

Dean reviewed the scans again, not believing what he was seeing, the level of complexity of the cybernetics beneath the gleaming metal that covered Bron's replacement limbs. There was only one planet this could have come from, only one group of sentients. It seemed impossible, and yet…

Dean had just found the most valuable cybernetic specimen in the galaxy. The one thing that Norem would trade anything to acquire—even Hayley. All Dean had to do was secure Bron.

Breathing much more evenly, Dean placed his hand on a control panel and let his fingers morph, integrating with the ship's systems. He signaled the nanites to stand by.

He needed a plan. Something that couldn't fail.

The Cygnian cyborg would be his.

Chapter One

The crystalline walls of the *Arrow* vibrated beneath Bron's feet as he ran toward the common room. Each blare of the ship's alarm sent a pulse of rainbow hues over the milky white surfaces surrounding him. What was wrong this time? Considering how many battles his prism—the band of Cygnian warriors he was part of—had been involved in lately, Bron did not know what to expect.

His prism was guarding what remained of a recently destroyed Tau Ceti base, attempting to figure out technology beyond anything they had ever seen before. They had been involved in taking out a Centauran vessel with vastly different, though just as advanced technology. A group of agents had targeted them in an attempt to bring the Cygnians into the war between the Coalition of Planets and the Tau Centauran Assembly.

For a group that was supposed to remain neutral, Bron and his fellow warriors had been involved in a great deal of events that could shape the future of galactic affairs. They had even dealt with the Cygnian 'Goddess,' who had turned out to be an alien entity meddling with them from an alternate plane of existence.

He knew these events should be at the forefront of his mind, but he was most concerned with an act of sabotage by a Scorpiian operative that had resulted in the loss of the *Reckoning*, one of the Coalition's last remaining warships. Bron had been flying his personal fighter through the area, bringing a lockbox to his brother, Dorn. The explosion had rocked his shard, sending it out of control, and resulted in the lockbox striking Bron's leg.

It wouldn't have been an issue if it had struck his right leg. Cygnians were nearly invulnerable once they reached maturity. Unfortunately, it had been his left—his cybernetic leg—and the lockbox had damaged it somehow.

Deep within his left calf, a burst of static crackled, coursing through his mechanical limb, almost as if it was answering the klaxon still blaring around him. Bron flailed his right arm to catch himself against the wall, using his natural limb to keep his balance as his cybernetic leg twitched uncontrollably. He didn't trust his left arm to be any better.

Not now…

His spine plates snapped up and a current of energy pulsed through him unlike anything he'd ever felt. Were the biological parts of his body malfunctioning as well? The tingling spread out from his spine plates and over his back and coursed down his right side—everywhere that he was still organic and not machine. His hearts pounded with a bruising, erratic rhythm, the left one adding an extra twinge as the biogel surrounding it cushioned the organ from the metal of his chest and back and all the intertwined mechanisms that had become part of him. He paused in the hallway, leaning against the wall as he tried to bring himself back under control.

A dull whine rose in his left ear as his cybernetics tried to power up. The rush of energy flooding his chest was electrifying his senses. Even with his eyes closed, he could see readouts of the ship's functions, locations of the other Cygnian warriors aboard the *Arrow*, results from the ship's scanners...

Something is out there.

Bron penetrated deeper into the *Arrow's* systems, linking his mind to the core computer. He reached out with the ship's scanner, as if brushing his fingers over the source of the odd readings. Whatever was out there, it had a disturbing texture. His biological senses translated it as oily and viscous. Bron wanted to recoil from the sensations, but he held himself steady, studying the data. The object was large, inorganic and hovering above the ground, much like the *Arrow*.

A cloaking field. Another ship.

He had to tell the others, but detaching from the *Arrow's* systems was like rising from tar. The bursts of static in his cybernetic systems complicated everything. Why was his body turning against him now? Bron's prism needed him. They should be able to count on him. He couldn't even count on himself.

"Any time, Bron." Rom's voice sounded over the ship's communication channel. Though his tone kept his perpetual teasing edge, Bron could sense Rom's concern.

Sharing a warrior's soul bond allowed the seven Cygnians of their prism to sense each other's emotions when they were strong enough. Whatever had caused the *Arrow's* proximity alarm to go off, it had Rom worried. Bron only hoped that Rom couldn't sense the concern clouding Bron's own emotions.

The static-like bursts from his leg subsided, though his spine plates remained erect. He checked his left arm to make sure the hologram that his wristbands continually projected over his cybernetics to conceal them was in place. Only blue skin was visible. Bron pushed away from the wall, then sprinted the rest of the distance to the common room. He slid to a stop when he arrived.

Tobek stood in the center of the large, circular space, staring at a holodisplay of the *Arrow* as it hovered deep within the dwarf planet that Earthlings had named Ceres. The celestial body drifted in the asteroid belt between Mars and Jupiter and had been the perfect spot for the Tau Ceti to create a secret base where they could experiment on humans and other unfortunate beings. Beings such as Tobek himself.

Through the transparent, pale-blue images of the

hologram, Bron could distinctly see Tobek's own modifications. The metal of the former Tau Ceti soldier's cybernetics gleamed in the light. Tobek had lost his right arm. It had been *taken* from him. As horrific as Bron's own experiences had been in becoming a cyborg, Tobek's were infinitely worse. Bron had suffered an accident during a beryl beast hunt. Tobek had been intentionally dismembered and experimented on by one of his own people, all in the name of creating a better soldier.

Norem, the scientist behind Tobek's modifications, hadn't just turned him into a cyborg. He had somehow modified Tobek's DNA, infusing it with Cygnian genetic material. Not even the ultra-advanced technology of Peri and Cyan, the Vegans who were working with Bron's group, could determine how Norem had turned Tobek into a Tau-Cygnian hybrid.

Regardless of how it had been done, Tobek was one of them now. All the warriors in the prism had accepted him as a fellow brother-in-arms.

"We could use Dorn's help with this," Tobek said. "He knows the security scans better than anyone."

"Dorn needs to use his security expertise to ensure the safety of his soulmate's family," Bron said.

Dorn was with two other members of their prism on Earth, Lar and Kral. They had found their soulmates in three sisters when agents of the Assembly targeted the sisters' family. The youngest, Amy, had almost been killed.

Dorn and the others were spending time with their soulmates' family and getting them settled in a new, more secure home in Harbor, Kansas. Aliens had secretly colonized the town, and it was the new primary base of operations for Earth's Department of Homeworld Security.

While Dorn was away, it was Bron's job to interpret security scans—something he'd already done with his own cybernetic technology. The trouble was, no one currently on the ship was supposed to know that Bron was a cyborg at all, let alone that the technology within him was the most advanced in the known galaxies. Only Dorn, Bron's biological brother, was aware of his cybernetics. The Psiarae, the aliens who had saved his life, were incredibly secretive and isolationist. They didn't even want anyone to know for certain that they existed, let alone that they had helped another group of sentients.

"What's going on?" Bron asked, as if he didn't already know.

"We're trying to figure out what that is." Tobek pointed at the holodisplay, where the light illuminated a faint silhouette. A very large silhouette.

"Bad news is, I think it's a ship." Rom's voice came over the comms from his station in the cockpit. "Good news is, they haven't tried to blow us up."

"Yet," Tobek added.

Tobek reached out to the holodisplay, rotating it to give Bron a better view. Big as it was, the outline of the vessel was smaller than the *Arrow*. It wouldn't be able to house a very large crew. Maybe two or three people could live on it. The ship was hovering nose-to-nose with the *Arrow*, almost as if it was taunting them.

The holodisplay flickered, then expanded to display a hologram of Rom and Tarn. Tarn was hunched over as if working on a control panel, though they couldn't see what he was interacting with. Rom was standing with his arms outstretched. Bron was certain his clasped hands were on the flight controls for the Arrow, ready to respond if whatever this was became aggressive. Nuar was the only one not displayed, though Bron was certain he and his soulmate, Lian, were viewing everything from the medbay. Confirming his thoughts, Nuar's voice came over the comm.

"Anybody else have a bad feeling about this?" Nuar said.

Tarn shrugged. "We can lead them away if we have to. Take them on a merry chase, as the Earthlings say."

"Peri and Cyan are still within the base," Rom said. "We can't leave them."

"Or the other two Tau-Cygnian cyborgs still in stasis in Norem's lab," Tobek added.

Bron nodded curtly, his attention transfixed on the faint outline of the ship. Something about it held his attention beyond the threat it presented. He struck the shining silver crystal of his wristbands together, making a high chime, then added his own voice to the sound. Humming a few different commands, he brought up a readout of the *Arrow's* scans superimposed over the holodisplay of the ship in front of him. He couldn't bring himself to look away from it for a moment.

"It's definitely a ship," Bron said.

"As they so eloquently say on Earth, 'Duh,'" Rom said. Tarn snickered.

"Could you please focus?" Nuar's voice was much more tense.

Of the four Cygnian warriors who remained on the *Arrow*, he was the only one who had found his soulmate. They needed to protect Lian as fiercely as they knew she would protect them. Bron's spine plates vibrated, his need to protect Nuar and Lian's soulmate bond momentarily overwhelming him. Where had that come from?

A targeting array appeared in his field of view, the bull's-eye flitting around the common room, looking for an enemy. Bron took a deep breath and let it out slowly, willing his emotions to calm. He couldn't lose control, even for a moment. Not only would that risk exposure, it could also endanger everyone near him.

"The ship's cloak isn't at full power," Tarn said.

Tobek looked over at Tarn's holographic avatar. "What does that mean?"

"It means they're letting us see them," Rom said. "They want us to know they're here."

"Why?" Tobek asked.

"They probably think they're taunting us," Bron said.

Tarn snorted, his tone thick with contempt. "As if a ship exists that could harm the *Arrow*."

Almost all known weaponry would glance off the crystalline structure of most Cygnian ships, but Tarn's kind of overconfidence was why Bron had suffered his injuries as a child. He wasn't willing to risk the safety of his prism or their soulmates. He stepped forward to scrutinize the holodisplay of the ship. Something about it was familiar.

"Not many ships have cloaks that we can't penetrate," Tarn said. "Vegans, Lyrians, and Scorpiians."

"You think this might be Dean?" Rom asked.

The vibration of Bron's spine plates increased. Dean had been behind the attack on Kral, Lar, and Dorn's soulmates' family. The Scorpiian had worked with Norem at this base. He had ordered Lian's abduction via the Centauran ship. Everything negative they had been through lately, Dean had played a part in.

It had been Dean's lockbox that had damaged Bron's systems.

Tarn nodded. "We'd be fools not to consider it."

"He is one of the few people who knows this base exists," Tobek said. "It was always a matter of 'when' he would show up to check on it, never 'if.'"

"And we know we have something he wants," Rom said.

Tarn nodded again. "The lockbox."

A shock of static crackled through Bron's leg. He held himself rigidly still so that the others wouldn't see his discomfort, doing everything in his power to shut down his emotions as well. The nanites the Psiarae had infused his body with were supposed to repair any damage to the mechanisms they had built for him. The nanites hadn't been able to repair whatever the lockbox had done. Bron had considered asking Tarn to examine him, but that would mean telling him secrets that Bron wasn't able to share. The Cygnian queen herself had ordered Bron to safeguard the Psiarae's secret. While Dorn knew of Bron's cybernetics, he lacked the skill to be of any help.

A yellow light flickered next to him, hovering within the holodisplay to let him know the communications array was receiving an incoming message. Someone was hailing them, and with Lar off the ship, it fell to Bron to deal with it. At least Rom would do most of the actual talking. Bron glanced over at Rom, who dropped his hands to his sides, then nodded.

"Let's see who we're dealing with," Rom said.

Chapter Two

Olivia had lost her mind. That was the only plausible explanation for why she had whisked herself and one of her best friends off the planet, asking him for the biggest favor she'd ever begged of anyone. She had been so desperate in her quest, she hadn't even stopped to arrange for someone to watch her Newfoundland, Zorro. She had never dreamed she would take her dog on an adventure in space.

"This is absolutely crazy," she murmured.

All of this trouble just so she could track down the few Cygnian warriors who weren't on Earth. Well, she was only interested in one. She didn't even know *which* one.

Her friend Zemanni stood out of sight of the large viewscreen embedded in the wall in the center of his ship's command room. His hand was resting on a small silver panel next to him. Actually, it looked more like it was fused to the panel than resting on it. His skin had turned the same silver as that part of the wall and seemed to meld with the metal as it swirled in place. He cocked his head and smirked.

"I just muted you," he said. "You were already connected to their comm channel."

Crap.

"How was I supposed to know?" she whispered, gesturing toward the viewscreen. "I thought the screen would light up or something to let me know they could hear me."

"We only see them if they let us see them," Zemanni said. "Right now, they're audio only, but they can see and hear you."

"You mean they've been watching me whispering to you like some kind of unhinged—"

Zemanni's smirk deepened. "I'm unmuting you now."

"Wait, what?" Olivia's mouth dropped open. She tried to say something to Zemanni—she wasn't even sure what —but only a few garbled words and some hissing 'S's escaped as she gestured frantically for him to mute her again. She wasn't ready for this. What had she been thinking, leaving Earth to chase after some weird feeling that might be nothing at all?

No, it wasn't nothing. It was everything. The other half of her soul was on that Cygnian ship, and she was going to find it—and the guy walking around with it.

"Is everything okay?" someone said over the comm system. The man's voice was pleasant and strong.

Olivia closed her eyes for a moment, trying to compose herself and calm her racing heart. She plastered on a huge smile and stood straighter, clasping her hands in front of her chest.

"Yes, yes. Everything's fine." She glared at Zemanni. He arched an eyebrow in response. Dropping her arms to her sides, she said, "Everything is fine," with greater confidence. She hoped.

"You look nervous," the man said.

So much for hope.

"Right, you can see me." More quietly, she said, "Of course, they can see me."

Zemanni was chuckling off screen, one hand over his mouth. She narrowed her eyes at him briefly, plotting her revenge. Switching his favorite coffee with decaf might be a little extreme, but she was considering it. The Scorpiian was the biggest coffee addict she'd ever met.

"I am a bit nervous." Bringing her attention back to the screen, she smiled. "It's my first time in outer space. I've never been off the planet before."

She had never wanted to leave Earth, but when that shuttle had flown over her head and her spine lit up like the Fourth of July on steroids, she knew she had to find out who had been inside. Whoever it was, she was certain he was her soulmate. Exactly how could she just come out and say that? It sounded crazy, even in her head.

Had he sensed her, too? She wasn't sure. If he had, why hadn't he flown his ship back to her? He could have done so if he'd wanted to. Maybe the pull he felt toward her

wasn't as strong as what she felt toward him. Maybe...
Maybe he could sense that she wouldn't be the soulmate
he wanted—that his people needed.

If their priority was repopulating their planet... Her
heart raced faster, her palms sweating. Old hurts rose, so
painful, they tightened her throat and threatened to silence
her. She wouldn't let them. Whatever was going on,
whatever her soulmate thought of her, she had to at least
meet him. She coughed to clear her throat, but the man
spoke before she could.

"It's considered polite to let others see your ship when
you're approaching a vessel," he said. "Just letting you
know, since you're new and all."

"Well, on Earth, it's considered polite to let people see
you if you can see the person you're talking to," she said.

"Fair enough."

The viewscreen lit up. Olivia's eyes hungrily searched
for the man she was looking for. Somehow, she knew the
Cygnian front-and-center was not her guy. He was
gorgeous—the same blue as a summer sky. A fine coat of
stubble covered his movie-star jaw, and his dark blue hair
fell down to his shoulders. He reached up to sweep his
bangs away from his bright violet eyes, flexing his
impressive, lean bicep as he did.

Even if she didn't know Rom was the Cygnian with
violet eyes, his movements would have given him away.
He had earned something of a reputation as a player

among the single women of Harbor. Olivia could see the appeal, but wasn't interested. He wasn't the man who still had her spine tingling with awareness. The energy spread over her back and along her arms and legs. It had been growing since Zemanni had activated the viewscreen. Did that mean her soulmate could see her? Why wasn't he saying anything?

Maybe he didn't like what he saw. Maybe he sensed that she... wasn't what he needed.

She stopped herself from reaching up to check her dark brown hair, rubbing her hands across the skirt of her dress instead. Should she have changed before heading after him? She was still in her favorite sundress, with its pale flower pattern, full skirts, tight bodice, and spaghetti straps. She loved how the yellow fabric looked against her brown skin. It was her favorite for a reason.

Was she too skinny? Her ex used to say that all the time. Right until he left, after—

She shook herself, letting her smile fade. This was who she was. The Cygnian she was looking for needed to accept her for that. And if he couldn't, then she didn't care if he was her soulmate. She would kick him to the curb and keep living her best life as the librarian for Earth's only city where aliens could visit without hiding their presence on the planet.

"So, how long do we stare at each other?" Rom smirked. "I mean, not that I'm unused to Earth females staring."

Olivia grimaced, but then laughed. "Yeah, I heard you were a charmer."

"Glad my reputation precedes me."

Oh, that cocky smile. No wonder half the town of Harbor was in love with him.

"Well, I showed you mine," he said. "You gonna show me yours?"

Her eyebrows rose, and she started stammering again. Why was it so much easier to talk in books? Her friend Nancy was the queen of witty repartee. Even Lian could hold her own in a conversation much better than Olivia.

"I... Uh... It's not my ship to show," she said. "I caught a ride with a friend."

"Just in the neighborhood, huh?" Rom said.

"Well, no, not..." She shook her head. "I was looking for... For... Lian. I'm Olivia. Did I say that already? No, I don't think so. Anyway, I wanted to see her, and thought I would surprise her with a visit."

Rom's smile faded. "Olivia. She's mentioned you. But how did you know where to find us?"

Crap.

Someone was about to get in trouble. Olivia wouldn't lie and say that Lian had told them where to find her. All that she had told Olivia and Nancy was that she was safe, she was with her soulmate, and they were working on something that she couldn't talk about. Some important technology or something. Olivia had been so desperate to reach her soulmate, fearing that he was leaving Earth and she'd never find him again. She hadn't thought this through.

When Zemanni showed up at the library as Olivia was trying to figure out what to do, it had seemed like fate. She had told him everything and asked for help. He'd simply responded with, "Come on," and led her to his ship. He hadn't even complained that she brought along her dog. She hadn't thought to ask how he knew where the Cygnians were or so much about what they were doing here. They were probably going to be angry. Scorpiians weren't exactly on most species' list of favorite people.

Before she could figure out a plan, Zemanni stepped forward and came to stand next to her.

"I brought her," he said.

No decaf for him. He was getting the best beans she could get her hands on once they were back on Earth. He cast one of the most condescending smirks she had ever seen in her life at the guy on the screen.

"And I don't think you need to ask how I knew where you were," Zemanni said.

"Zemanni, be nice," Olivia hissed in a whisper.

"Scorpiians don't play nice," Rom said, a growl reverberating through his words. "And if you know what's good for you, you'll—"

"She'll what?" Zemanni broke in. "Throw herself out

of an airlock? She brought along her dog. Want him to do a spacewalk, too?"

Zorro must have picked up on the word 'walk,' because he let out a loud bark. He ran into the room from wherever he'd been sleeping, then leapt up on Olivia with his paws on her shoulders.

"No one is doing a spacewalk." Zorro muffled her words as he tried to lick her face. She should have chosen different ones, because he started barking again.

What had gotten into him? An answering 'woof' sounded from the viewscreen. Ed, Lian's Saint Bernard, must be in the room with Rom. Where was Lian, though? Usually, those two were inseparable.

"Listen, we're not about to trust a—" Rom stopped as someone stepped partially into frame. Olivia could only see part of one huge, muscled arm, his skin the same blue as a washed out winter sky.

"Drop your cloak and land." His much deeper voice came over the comms.

The tingling in Olivia's spine amped up a million degrees. Her breath quickened, her heart pounding in her chest. Zorro paced back and forth in front of the viewscreen, whining. She craned her neck as if she could see around the edges of the monitor.

"Why… What…" It took her a moment to realize that words were coming out of her mouth. She shook her head and said, "Who are you?"

"This is Bron." Rom arched an eyebrow at the Cygnian next to him, then stepped aside.

The newcomer turned, entering the viewscreen's field —filling it. She glimpsed a long row of spine plates standing straight out from his back, vibrating quickly enough to blur their edges. His short hair was dark blue, almost black, and a striking contrast to his pale blue skin. His shoulders and chest were so broad they filled the screen. Enormous muscles rippled along his arms and strained the white fabric of his tunic. His square jaw was just as muscled, his dark brow lowered over electric-blue eyes that glowed brighter as he looked at her.

Bron...

The hairs on Olivia's arms rose and her spine erupted in waves of tingling pleasure that spread over her back, curling around her abdomen and pooling deep in her belly. This man—this Cygnian warrior—was her soulmate. She knew it in her bones.

What she didn't understand was why he didn't look happy to see her.

Chapter Three

Bron's hearts increased their painful pounding in his chest. He wondered how much the biogel could handle. The hologram of the beautiful Earthling mesmerized him. Her dark hair whispered across her slender shoulders and flowed down her back. She wore a yellow dress that clung to her chest and hugged her slight waist, flowing around her long legs. The fabric highlighted the golden tones of her sepia brown skin. Her features were so delicate. She reminded him of the most intricate crystalline sculptures crafted by the greatest masters of the Cygnian arts—except she was even more beautiful.

As he stared into her dark onyx eyes, he knew he had never and would never after see anyone or anything more beautiful in his life than this woman. He desperately wanted to reach out and touch her, to run his fingertips across the angle formed where her jaw met her slender neck. To press a kiss behind her ear as he whispered his eternal devotion to her.

But then... Then, she would lift her hands to his shoulders and run her fingertips down along his arms. She would feel what he was. The hologram projected by his wristbands could only change his appearance. She would know the truth—that he had become something more than just a Cygnian. Something... else. And then she would uncover the secret he had sworn to keep.

Of all the soulmates the universe could have gifted him with, why this one? This woman who was utter perfection, whose gentle eyes made him want to fall to his knees before her, made his hearts want to leap from his chest.

Would he be able to control himself with her? His hearts were pounding and his skin felt electrified. The sensation spread through his mechanical limbs, overpowering the static that had plagued him. The cabling and synthetic synaptic pathways of his cybernetics flooded with energy, nearly overwhelming him with the need to move, to eliminate everything between them, to shatter the crystal of their ship and launch himself toward her. Bron drew on every ounce of his self-control to shut down his emotions, to see this as a curiosity, just another scientific situation for him to analyze, parse, and file away in his memory.

The holodisplay depicted not only her, but the others in the room with her, as real as if they were sharing the space with Bron. The optical readout in his cybernetic cortex allowed him to see that only Ed, Tobek, and himself were actually in the room, though it seemed to be filled with life forms. An enormous dog paced before Olivia's holographic avatar, looking up at what must be the viewscreen on their ship and whining, as if it wanted to reach them. Lian's dog, Ed, was standing nearby, his head held at a curious angle. Bron's studies of the creatures made him certain Ed was attempting to sort out the data he was receiving from his eyes and what he wasn't receiving from his nose.

The dog didn't disturb Bron. No, the assassin staring at them, his arms crossed casually over his chest, commanded Bron's attention.

Bron looked toward the Scorpiian and repeated, "Drop your cloak and land. We'll generate a shield to hold in an atmosphere breathable by Earthlings and that will block harmful radiation."

"That's great," Olivia said, her light voice sending shivers along Bron's spine plates. He didn't think they would ever rest against his back again after this. "It'll be great to see… Lian."

Bron sensed the truth. She was here to see *him*, her soulmate. That was something he could not encourage. If he kept her away, he risked backlash from the soulmate bond that could cause his death. That was preferable to taking the chance that he might lose control and hurt her.

"Tarn will make the arrangements." Bron struck his wristbands together and hummed the note that shut down the holodisplay in the common room, closing the communication channel as well. He stared across the space that suddenly seemed much emptier with only himself, Tobek, and Ed.

How was Bron going to handle this? If Olivia was his soulmate, the desire to touch would be hard-wired into both of them. If she touched him in the wrong place, she'd notice his cybernetics. He would just have to keep her at a distance, physically as well as emotionally. That didn't mean he couldn't take care of her. Whether or not she realized it, she was not safe with that Scorpiian. Bron had to get her off that ship.

He hurried down the corridor to the hatch at the underside of their ship, confident that Tarn would have everything ready since he'd been listening to the communication. As expected, his friend was waiting near the controls.

"We better hurry and get Olivia on board," Tarn said. "With how antsy Lian has been lately, she's likely to throw herself from the hatch to greet her. I'm surprised she didn't force Nuar to let her say something while you guys were talking."

"Lian is still adjusting to life aboard the *Arrow*," Bron said.

"Then why is she getting worse? She used to be fine with everything. Well, what little we saw of her." A purple tinge came to Tarn's cheeks, and he looked away.

Lian and Nuar had spent most of their time 'bonding' in Nuar's quarters. All the Cygnians who had found their soulmates had done so. The urge to be close, to forge unity between their souls, was impossible to deny. Lar had tried to resist the link and had died for it. Luckily, his soulmate was too stubborn to let him go, as was he, when he realized he could fight to return to her through their bond.

"The corridor's shielding is set, I'm projecting artificial gravity within that matches Earth's, and I've sent a notification to the Scorpiian vessel." Tarn glanced over at Bron with his deep indigo eyes. "You ready for this? We don't know if we can trust them."

"We can trust Olivia."

"You seem pretty sure of that."

Bron knew Tarn was searching for information. Bron was adept at keeping his thoughts to himself after years of practice and took care to ensure he let nothing slip now. He struck his wristbands together, a high chime resonating in the space as they activated, then he hummed the note to create a pocket of breathable atmosphere around himself, just in case. The hatch opened before them and Bron leapt the twenty feet to the ground.

Across the cavern, her skin gleaming in the shimmering golden light from the energy encasing the safe corridor, Olivia stood next to the biggest dog Bron had ever seen. Her eyes grew wide as she stared at him, her delicate lips twitching into the slightest smile.

More tingles of energy flooded over his body, testing his control. He pushed his emotions deeper, locking them away within himself and focusing on the pulses of the mechanical signals always murmuring in the background of his awareness. The familiar hum could barely mask the keen desire threatening to well up within him, the urge to run to her and take her in his arms.

Her dog was having no such luck controlling himself. 'Zorro,' she had called him, began barking, then lurched forward, pulling Olivia behind him. She ran to keep up with the black-furred animal. The dog was pulling the arm that held his lead straight in front of her as she tried to match his pace. Bron quickly walked forward, though he didn't dare let himself run. Tarn cast an odd look toward Bron as he ran past, reaching the pair first. He reached down to the dog, trying to help calm him.

"Whoa, there," Tarn said, kneeling to embrace the animal. "Settle down."

Zorro whined, looking back and forth between Tarn and Bron. When Bron arrived, the dog sat and leaned his head against Tarn's chest as the other Cygnian stroked his fur. His tail whipped the ground in a frantic beat that reminded Bron of the thunderous drumming of his own hearts.

Olivia stared up at Bron, her large eyes filled with a warmth that seemed to seep into him. He longed to reach out and stroke the delicate curve of her neck, to trace his thumb across the soft line of her jaw. He was drifting forward, the world around them vanishing until she was all he could see. Her lips parted as she stepped toward him as well.

In his perception, waves of light flowed over her skin, the cybernetic implants in his mind recording every detail about her. He tried to shut them down, to keep seeing her with his own eyes, but a sudden flashing red light caught his attention, drawing his focus down their protective corridor. Zemanni leaned against his ship, arms crossed over his chest as he watched their group.

Bron's power supplies ramped up, flooding his mechanical limbs with energy. His left leg sent another pulse of static through his awareness. He locked down the muscles in his face to keep from wincing. Stepping around Olivia, he placed himself between the Scorpiian and his soulmate. Tarn rose to his feet, one hand clinging to Zorro's collar.

"Relax," Zemanni said. "I just wanted you to see me."

"Why?" Bron asked.

"Scorpiians can do a lot of things, but even I can't be in two places at once," Zemanni said. "This way, you see Olivia and Zorro and know that I am not either of them."

Bron would never mistake Olivia for anyone else. He knew her soul, could sense it within her, through their connection. Zorro would have concerned him, but Bron planned to scan the dog when they went on board—and would still do so. He could take no chances with his soulmate. Another frisson of static coursed up his leg, reminding him that he himself might be a danger to her.

"We've seen you," Tarn said. "Now leave."

"There's no need to be rude." Olivia stepped aside so that Bron was no longer blocking her view of Zemanni— nor Zemanni's view of her.

Zemanni shrugged one shoulder, pushing off from his ship as the hatch slid open next to him. "Don't worry about it. But know that I'll be around. I'm her ride, after all, and I don't leave friends behind." He stepped into his ship, the hatch closing behind him.

Friends. The thought made Bron's spine plates vibrate fiercely.

"We better get back on board the *Arrow*," Tarn said. "I don't enjoy being out here in a corridor connected to his ship."

"Zemanni is my friend," Olivia said forcefully.

"Scorpiians don't have friends. They have missions and bounties." Bron turned and headed toward the open hatch at the underside of their ship. The others followed, Olivia walking at a brisk pace to keep up.

"Maybe none of the Scorpiians you know have friends, but he *is* mine," she said. "Please show him some respect."

His hearts surged with rage, activating his cybernetic battle sequence. Targeting arrays dotted his field of vision, dizzying him with their frenetic movements as they sought something to analyze for attack. Bron took a deep breath and let it out as surreptitiously as he could. Showing respect for a Scorpiian? He would sooner dive into one of Earth's oceans. He suppressed a shudder at the thought of his body's density, pulling him down into their dark depths.

Bron turned to regard Olivia and took in the blazing passion in her eyes. She meant every word—truly believed that Zemanni was her friend. Was his soulmate a fool? Bron couldn't believe it. But if she wasn't being tricked, did that mean that Zemanni was a Scorpiian worthy of friendship and all that entailed? It was hard for Bron to accept.

Her presence overwhelmed his senses, impairing his judgment. Bron needed space and time to process everything he had learned, to adjust to being near her. They hadn't even touched, and his already off-kilter systems were responding in ways he couldn't control.

"I'll take the dog." Bron knelt next to Zorro and picked up the enormous animal. He tried not to notice the wave of hurt and confusion that crossed Olivia's face and flowed out from her through their bond.

Tarn's eyebrows rose. He glanced back and forth between them, then said, "Okay. If I may?"

Gesturing with his arms outstretched, he waited for Olivia to nod before pulling her close to his chest and then leaping up into the ship. Bron gave himself one more moment—one more deep, calming breath as he tried to bring himself back under control. Holding Zorro firmly, he made the leap.

Chapter Four

What was going on? Bron was her soulmate. Olivia was sure of it. From the moment she saw him, her heart had beat faster, her skin had felt electrified, and her spine was alight with energy. She wanted more than anything to run to him, throw her arms around his neck, hold on, and never let go. He was supposed to feel the same way. So, why did he have Tarn bring her into the ship? Why would Bron not come near her?

Lian had told Olivia stories about the other soulmates. She knew that resisting the bond could kill a Cygnian. Lar had resisted and actually died. They had brought him back using a mix of Earth medical techniques, Cygnian technology, and honestly, what sounded like straight-up magic. His soulmate, Sophie, had held on tight enough to their bond to help him pull himself back to his body. What could hold Bron back to where he would risk such a fate? Olivia was supposed to be feeling everything Bron felt, at least emotionally. All she sensed was that maddening pull.

She followed Bron silently as they headed for wherever Lian was. Probably the medical bay. Olivia suppressed a shiver, reminding herself that this was an alien spaceship, not a human hospital. It would be different. There would be nothing to trigger her. Still, her heart raced. She wiped her palms on her dress, trying to calm herself.

A deep dread rose in her. Could Bron sense… Did he know…

She shook her head sharply. She wasn't any less because of how she was. And she hadn't even checked with the Vegans yet to see if they could help her. The hospital in Harbor that the small, reptilian aliens had created for their community was incredibly advanced within, but appeared normal from the outside. The Vegans weren't ready to share with the rest of the world that aliens were real and had settled on Earth. Olivia still wasn't ready to go into a building that brought up so many horrible memories.

Zorro had run ahead the moment Bron set him down. They found him in a large, circular room, flopped on the milky white floor on his back right next to Ed. The St. Bernard's mouth hung open in a doggy smile that matched Zorro's.

At least someone is happy to see us.

Tarn broke off from their group, nodding toward her. "I know you say Zemanni is your friend, but I think we'll all feel better with me in engineering while there's a Scorpiian vessel nose-to-nose with us."

Olivia barely stopped herself from letting out a

frustrated groan. Pulling herself straighter, she said, "Do what you have to do. I promise, he's no threat to you."

Tarn started to speak, but then stopped himself. He merely smiled instead. He turned and headed down one of the corridors that led away from the room. Olivia stared after him for a moment. What would happen now that she was alone with Bron? Would he turn to her and explain what was going on?

"Lian is this way." Bron's deep, rumbling voice sent a shiver coursing along Olivia's spine.

Guess not.

"Thank you," she said, keeping her head high as she walked toward him.

The corridor wasn't wide, and he wasn't too far away. She angled her walk so that she would pass close by, giving him a chance to reach out to her, to say or do anything that might make it seem he recognized her as his soulmate. As she neared, he shrank back, brushing the wall with his shoulder. It was like he wanted to put as much distance between them as possible. The energy arching along her spine intensified. The entire right half of her body erupted in goosebumps, and she felt almost as if she was leaning toward him, though she was standing straight. It was as if her soul was reaching out and being rejected.

Again.

Tears flooded her eyes. She wanted to harden her heart against him, but that just wasn't in her nature. Instead, she let the pain flow through her, accepting it, thanking it for letting her know she needed to be careful with this person. Soulmate or not, he was not to be trusted. He would hurt her. Just as her ex had.

At least Bron didn't start something and abandon me when I needed him most.

Everyone had a reason for being who they were, for making the choices they made. She didn't know Bron at all. After this... coldness coming from him, she wasn't sure she wanted to. Maybe being soulmates didn't make them perfect for each other. Maybe she was destined to be alone.

She quickened her steps, as if she could outpace the memories threatening to suffocate her. Her heart beat faster, the surrounding hall almost spinning. Blinking her eyes to clear them, she focused on getting to Lian. To someone she *could* trust. Even if she was in a medical bay. More memories pushed at Olivia's awareness, threatening to send her into a panic. She had to get ahold of this, had to bring herself back under control.

"Olivia..." Bron groaned out her name with so much pain and longing, Olivia gasped.

She stopped, turning to face him with her hand over her heart as if to hold it back. His jaw was tight, the muscles standing out beneath his short-cropped beard. He narrowed his eyes in what looked like pain, a deep furrow between his brows. He was holding his left arm with his right hand, clutching it tight.

Was he having a heart attack? Did Cygnians even have heart attacks?

Her few years of nursing school came rushing back to her. Olivia pushed aside her own needs and focused on the person in front of her who needed help.

"Stay calm," she said, stepping closer with her arms raised in what she hoped was a peaceful gesture. "I'm going to help you."

He shook his head and backed up a step. "You can't."

Okay, now he was just making her mad. Whatever they did or didn't have between them, she was not about to stand by and let someone suffer if there was anything she could do about it.

"Oh, is that what you think?" she said, marching forward and reaching for him.

Bron still tried to back away from her, but his left leg gave a weird spasm and he fell toward the wall instead. He landed hard on his shoulder. Rainbows of opalescence rippled out from the milky white surface of the crystal wall where he impacted. He closed his eyes, breathing fast through his nose, his mouth clenched tight. Something was very wrong. Was this the result of rejecting their bond? Olivia didn't think it would manifest so quickly.

How did someone even check vitals on a Cygnian? She wished that the videos her town made about the alien visitors who came to Harbor included medical facts.

Would it hurt Bron if she touched him? He was acting as if it would. Or maybe he was just being a baby and didn't want the commitment of a soulmate. That was more her luck with guys. If that was so, he was in for a treat, because she had no intention of pursuing anything with him aside from giving him whatever medical care she could until she could call for help.

Best to keep it basic, since she had no idea what she was doing. Check his temperature and compare it to Tarn. The other Cygnian's arms had been cooler than she expected, so if Bron felt warm, that would be... information. Check his pulse...es, since she was pretty sure Cygnians had similar heart rates to humans, given that their heartbeats would shift to match that of their soulmates after they fully bonded, according to Lian.

Olivia reached out and pressed one hand to his forehead and the other to what would be a major pulse point on his neck. A brief electric zap stung her skin where they touched. Then a wave of sensation hit her like a tsunami, energy blasting down her arms and flooding her body. She gasped as her skin rose in goosebumps, her spine lighting up with electric pleasure that coursed through her. An instant inferno bloomed in every nerve, pooling deep in her belly and making her core throb.

But with the pleasure also came intense pain. Not physical, but emotional. The feelings flooded her with just as much intensity, stealing her breath away and bringing fresh tears to her eyes. So many emotions, it was hard to sort through them. Longing, adoration, and even awe. He looked at her and saw a goddess. But lurking behind it was bitterness stronger than she had ever felt. Bitterness and shame, somehow tied in with threads of gratitude that only made the emotions worse. And at the base of them all, a deep belief that she would be better off without him.

Bron groaned, but the lines around his eyes eased. He shook his head, not to dislodge her touch, but as if denying something. Denying himself this?

"Whatever it is, I don't care," she whispered in a breathless voice. "Whatever is holding you back, don't let it."

His eyes snapped open, their brilliant blue spilling onto the surrounding walls. Her breath caught at the intensity of his gaze. Somehow, she could hold it, even though the light from them was dazzlingly bright. The furrow between his brows deepened, as did the lines at the edges of his eyes. She felt as though time had stopped around them, that they were on the precipice of a cliff, and if they leapt from it, they could fly—but only if they leapt together.

"It's okay," she said, softly. "It really is."

His breath rushed from him and he grabbed her, pulling her tight against his chest. His lips crashed down onto hers, ferocious and demanding. She gasped from the intensity of his passion, and he slid his tongue into her mouth, exploring every inch as if starved for her. Each stroke fed the energy building within her, coiling tighter in her core. He pulled up the fabric of her dress and grabbed her thighs, lifting her so that she could wrap her legs around his waist. She held tight to his shoulders as he turned so that he could press her against the wall, grinding his erections against her core. Something was... off. The feel of him beneath her hands. She couldn't sort through the sensations, a thick haze of lust clouding her thoughts.

Bron released her lips, but only to mark a blazing trail of need along her cheek and jaw, down to her neck. Everywhere he touched her, she was flame. He sucked on her skin hard, his fingers digging into her backside. The energy coursing along her spine felt like lightning, arcing out through her and bringing every cell in her body to life. He grunted with a frustration that she shared at the clothing that separated them. Her core tightened as he rubbed against her clit. He gently raked his teeth over her neck, panting along her skin.

"I can't," he murmured in a raspy voice. "I can't."

If she couldn't sense his need, his overwhelming desire for her, she might have panicked. But she knew he wanted her as much as she wanted him. Whatever was blocking her from feeling his emotions before was gone. As long as that connection remained, as long as he stayed open to her, they could work through anything else.

"You can," she said.

She gasped as he thrust against her, but sensed that wall rising within him again. Why was he trying to shut her out? Soulmate bonds were gifts from the universe. They were supposed to be perfect for each other in every way. Olivia had already believed in soulmates when Lian shared the wonders of finding her other half. Why didn't Bron believe, when it was a fundamental part of his people's spirituality?

Something else was holding him back. Making him doubt *himself*, not their bond. She remembered her own moment of doubt from earlier, fighting off her fear that he wouldn't be able to accept her. The same fear echoed in her heart from him. So, she told him the words that she needed to hear.

"I accept you," she said. "All of you. Just as you are."

Chapter Five

Bron shuddered as Olivia's sweet words flowed through his mind. How could she accept him when she didn't even know who or what he was? Didn't know about the secrets and lies he had to live with? His oath to Queen Ehmach bound him from telling anyone what he was—the only Cygnian cyborg ever to exist. Olivia would have to carry those burdens as well if they were to bond. That was, if she would even still want to.

Would Olivia feel the difference between the metal arm that held her and the biological one? She didn't seem to notice it. The metal was nearly as hard as his Cygnian skin and matched his skin temperature. If he kept his wristbands active, projecting the holographic field that made him appear the same as any other Cygnian, perhaps she would never know. But how could he keep such a thing from his soulmate? Especially when his cybernetics were malfunctioning?

It was hard enough keeping the secret from his warrior-brothers. Avoiding their touch had become second nature to Bron over the years. He was always careful to keep his right side toward everyone, just in case they bumped shoulders, which was a common custom among his people. Since his childhood, during challenges and playful sparring, he made sure others never grasped his left arm for long enough to realize it felt different beneath their hands. Over time, he became so skilled in battle, no one could touch him at all.

Touch was so important to a Cygnian, though. And Bron had never touched another like this, or been touched by another. He wanted more.

"Bron." Nuar's panicked voice came over the ship's comm system. "I need you in the medbay. Now."

Olivia's eyes widened. "Is Lian okay?"

There were no other humans on the ship. No one else who might need Nuar's help. But if something had happened that made Nuar require Bron's help...

Bron hummed a note that would open the communications channel where he stood. "We're on our way."

He stepped back from the wall as Olivia unclasped her legs from his waist. Her knees were unsteady, and he held her for a few moments while she regained her equilibrium. Thankfully, his own had returned during their kiss, the static burst that had afflicted him most recently subsiding. She shook her dress, letting it fall back into place.

"Come on." She reached for his left hand.

Instinctively, he jerked back, but softened his

movement into a sort of side-step where he could grasp her with his right hand. Her brow furrowed at the odd movement, confusion sweeping across her beautiful features. She shook herself, resolve chasing everything else away.

Bron led them to the medical bay, comforted by Olivia's warmth at his side. He would find a way to explain everything to her. Then he would discover if she truly could accept him.

When they reached the medbay, he pulled her behind him to shield her from any threats within. Without thinking, he issued a command to open the door directly to the ship's computer instead of using his wristbands. If Nuar noticed...

The door slid open, and his concern for Nuar noticing anything vanished. Nuar's full attention was on his soulmate. Lian was standing in the center of the room with her hands on her hips while Nuar stood a few feet away, his arms outstretched, as if he was preparing for her to attack him. Nuar's spine plates were upright, their edges blurred. The intense vibrations sent ripples of energy along the walls, flooding the milky crystal with rainbows.

"Lian, please let me examine you," he said.

"This is such bullshit." Lian threw her arms up in the air, then let them fall back to her sides. "Amy can see beyond the human spectrum and has that one super-strong arm. Sophie can electrocute people through an open communications channel and has those cool electric spine plates. And all I get is red eyes? I mean, they're cool-looking, but I was holding out for... I don't know, invulnerability or something."

"Lian..." Nuar's voice was taut with worry. He approached her slowly, keeping his arms outstretched before him.

"I'm sorry," she said, lifting her hands to her cheeks and wiping tears away. "This isn't me. This isn't me."

Finally, Nuar reached her and pulled her into his embrace. "We'll figure this out. Bron is here. He'll help."

"I'm here, too." Olivia stepped out from behind Bron, releasing her grip on him as she headed toward her friend. He forced himself to let her go, following a few paces behind.

"Oh my god, Olivia." Lian pushed away from Nuar, fanning her face with her hands as she ran to meet her friend.

She wrapped her arms around Olivia's waist as soon as she was within reach. Olivia returned the embrace, her eyes widening. A wave of concern flowed out from her. Though they hadn't fully bonded yet, Bron could already feel echoes of her emotions through their connection. Nuar was flooding the prism bond he and Bron shared with fear and desperation.

For a moment, Bron wondered how he would react if he suspected something was wrong with his Olivia. The thought nearly snapped what self-control he had put back in place since his lapse in the corridor. He pushed the thought away and focused on letting Nuar and Olivia's emotions pass through him, shielding his own. He couldn't afford to let such powerful feelings influence him.

"I'm so happy to see you," Lian said.

"I'm happy to see you, too." Olivia glanced over at Nuar, who stared at the pair with naked desperation. She rubbed Lian's back and asked, "What's going on with you, though?"

"I don't know," Lian practically howled. "Maybe I'm homesick."

Olivia's lips quirked into an odd grimace as she shook her head. Clearly, she didn't think that was the case. She looked over Lian's head, her keen scrutiny scanning the room. Lifting one of her arms, she spun her finger in a circle, then pointed at Lian, motioning for Nuar to come closer. She was mouthing something, but Nuar's focus was on Lian.

Bron let out a frustrated snort, then stepped closer. He struck his wristbands together and hummed a note to activate their scanning function, hoping he wouldn't have to use them for too long. Constantly running the holographic projectors to conceal his cybernetics was a drain on their energy, and he had to be sure to keep them charged enough to protect his secret.

Standing behind the women, Bron scanned Lian's body,

holding his arms out to get good readings. Olivia cast a grateful smile at him. Heat filled his chest, flooding down his abdomen and through the right side of his body. He did his best to ignore it, focusing on what he was doing instead.

"Let me see you," Olivia said, standing straighter.

Lian leaned back a bit and looked up at Olivia. Scarlet light accented Olivia's delicate features, sparkling and reflecting in her eyes.

"Wow, that does look cool." Olivia kept her voice gentle. "When did it happen?"

"I don't know," Lian said. "My eyes were kind of burning this morning and I came to ask Nuar if he had any eye drops and he like totally freaked out." She turned to glare at Nuar as she said the last part, seeming a bit more like her usual strong-willed self.

The warmth Olivia had brought forth in Bron chilled as he saw that Lian's eyes were now the same spectral red as Nuar's. They even glowed, as all Cygnians' eyes glowed when they felt intense emotion. Was it Bron's imagination, or was the skin around her eyes tinged with a bit of blue as well?

"Do you have any other symptoms?" Olivia asked.

"No," Lian snapped. "Well, yeah. I don't know, maybe?"

"Just tell me how you feel," Olivia said.

"I don't know!" Lian started to cry again. "Ugh, it's

like the worst PMS of my life! My emotions are all over the place and I'm so super itchy, I can't stand it. I'm tired all the time and so freaking bloated, my pants barely fit. Except that could be because I'm eating all the food in the universe and still ravenous and half the time what I eat makes me feel sick and this is all your fault!" She turned around, releasing Olivia and swatting at Nuar.

"I don't know what is happening, but I swear by the Goddess, I will do everything in my power to fix it," Nuar said, his voice pleading.

"It's your Goddess who caused this," Lian shouted. "She did that weird zappy thing and altered us all so we'd be more compatible."

Olivia's eyebrows rose. The most intense joy he had ever felt radiated from her like a sun, blasting through their connection. Her heart quickened, pulling the beats of his own along with it. Then, following the flood of happiness, a despair as dark as the void of space swept in after it. Olivia shook her head, pushing it away.

With the intensity of her emotions, Bron could clearly feel her compartmentalizing everything, bringing herself under control. He knew the feeling well. He just wasn't sure why she was doing it or what had caused either of the powerful emotions.

"Honey..." Olivia gripped Lian's arm gently and stepped in front of her. "Compatible how?"

"So we could have their babies or something," Lian

said.

Olivia smiled, slowly nodding her head, her eyebrows still high on her forehead. The joy was still bubbling beneath the surface. Wait, she didn't think...

"No." Lian shook her head. "No, no, no. There is no way... Oh my god. How am I going to tell my parents? We're not even married yet." She turned toward Nuar and yelled, "You said we'd need the Vegans' help! You said we didn't have to take measures to prevent it!"

"Prevent what?" Nuar said.

"Oh wow, this guy really is clueless," Olivia murmured.

Bron was catching on, though. His own hearts beat more strongly, a hope swelling within him he couldn't deny. Though it would drain his wristbands further, he activated a secondary holograph, projecting an image of Lian's scan for them all to see.

Her eyes were the easiest change to notice, but the scanners highlighted other systems that were undergoing massive metabolic and genetic changes. Energy coursed just under Lian's skin, restructuring it to increase its durability. Deeper, her bones were assimilating greater amounts of calcium, but also other minerals that would make them nearly unbreakable, as those of a Cygnian.

Lian and Nuar both looked at the scan, their eyes widening and features going lax with awe. They stepped closer. Bron hummed a note to enlarge the section of the scan that he knew had captured their interest.

In the center of Lian's belly, nestled within her womb, was a tiny, precious life.

The baby's blue skin was pale, but from the row of spine plates just beginning to emerge and his other readings, Bron could tell that this was a Cygnian. Human as well, but also Cygnian.

"Is that…" Nuar began. "Is that…"

"Hope for our people," Bron said. "This is your daughter."

Chapter Six

Lian burst into tears. She turned to Nuar, burying her face in his chest as she wrapped her arms around him. Olivia barely kept her own tears at bay. This was one of her best friends. Lian was having a baby with a man she loved.

A baby...

How could Olivia's heart hold so much joy and yet be shattering to pieces at the same time? She had trained for this as a nurse. Her own emotions would cloud her judgment of the situation and could lead to mistakes at crucial moments. She took a deep breath in through her nose and let it out as surreptitiously as she could through her mouth, pushing the emotions into an imaginary box and locking it. She would deal with them later. For now, she could allow herself to be happy for her friend, but not so much that it distracted her from helping.

Nuar looked stunned. He kept staring at the hologram, frozen in place. Olivia felt a little shudder as she remembered what Lian had told her about Lar. Cygnians turned into statues when they passed, and Lar had come dangerously close because of the emotional toll of denying his soulmate bond. Olivia would feel better seeing Nuar move.

"Now would be a good time to hold her back," Olivia prompted.

Nuar's arms rose to embrace Lian, though his amazed focus stayed rooted on the hologram. His skin paled and his eyes glowed a livid red. Behind him, his spine plates let out an even more intense vibration. The surrounding air rippled with a mirage-effect.

"Is she okay?" he asked.

"The baby seems healthy," Bron said, deactivating the hologram.

Bron stared at Olivia with an odd passive expression. Had he sensed her inner turmoil a moment ago? If so, why wasn't he trying to comfort her? Another pang shot through her. This wasn't going at all the way she had envisioned what it might be like if she also had a Cygnian soulmate the few times she'd let herself daydream about it. If it hadn't been for that moment in the hall, she could almost convince herself that their connection was all in her head. Bron's reaction to her ranged from arctic cold to volcanic. The vacillations were messing with her.

"I meant Lian." Nuar tightened his arms around his soulmate. "And how can you even know? There's never been a human-Cygnian hybrid before."

"Sorca is similar enough for us to use her biomarkers,"

Bron said.

"Sorca?" The name was familiar to Olivia, but she couldn't quite place it.

"Kral's sister," Bron said. "The High Council engineered her, infusing Cygnian DNA into Sadirian DNA. Sadirians are genetically almost identical to humans."

"That should help us with Lian," Olivia said.

"But they developed Sorca in a laboratory," Nuar said. "They grew her in a maturation chamber under controlled conditions. This is totally different." He shook his head, pulling Lian closer. "What do we do? How do we keep them both safe?"

Bron approached the couple, placing his right hand on Nuar's shoulder. The sweet gesture seemed odd somehow. He was angling his body away so that his left side was as far from Nuar as Bron could manage. What was going on with him?

"You may not wish to hear this now, but this is the will of the Goddess," Bron said. "Whatever else she is, she is still our Maker. She wants the Cygnians to continue. It wouldn't be logical for her to do so at the cost of our soulmates. You would die without each other."

"Thank you so much for your incredible sensitivity and comfort, Bron," Lian said, her voice dripping with sarcasm. "I get why you're the science officer and Lar is in charge of communications."

Bron's brow furrowed, and he stepped back. "I'm merely stating my observations and conclusions."

"I think what Bron is trying to say is that you don't need to worry," Olivia said. "You told me you and the other Earthlings who were in the room were altered by some incredibly powerful alien."

"Our Goddess," Bron said. "The Maker. We're still parsing through scans to determine how she altered all of us to increase our compatibility, hoping to continue our race."

Olivia tried to ignore the zing that went through her at the thought. If she had been there, would their Goddess have been able to help her, too? How disappointed would Bron be when he found out that Olivia wouldn't be able to help with repopulating their planet?

A spike of loss burst through her, breaking her tightly maintained control. Bron's eyebrows furrowed. She was sure he was sensing her emotions. Olivia tamped down her feelings, keeping her attention on Lian and Nuar. Since Nuar was the medic and this involved his soulmate, there was no way he could be objective. Bron had data, but his bedside manner was about the worst she'd ever seen.

"I'm sure whatever she did was to keep you safe during this." Olivia smiled down at Lian's tear-stained face. She reached out and rubbed Lian's back, saying, "Hey. This is a good thing. You're having a baby."

She tried to keep her voice gentle, but there was a hitch

to it that Lian picked up on. The fear in Lian's eyes turned to something even worse. Pity.

"Oh god, I'm so sorry," Lian said, pushing away from Nuar's chest so that she could hug Olivia. "Are you okay?"

"I'm fine," Olivia rasped. She cleared her throat, redoubling her efforts to keep her emotions under tight control. "Let's keep the focus on you and your sweet baby girl."

Lian leaned back enough to look into Olivia's eyes, an unspoken question passing between them. The iron cage Olivia had built around her heart buckled. She imagined chains whipping into place around it, with huge padlocks. The pain within her still rattled and fought for release. Her heart was pounding and her throat was so tight she could barely breathe.

Until what felt like a cool breeze rushed over her and through her. Blue crystal rose around the image in her mind, growing over the iron cage and reinforcing it. Soothing energy came with it, wrapping her heart in a warm embrace, telling her everything was going to be okay. That she wasn't alone.

She glanced at Bron to see him staring at her with an intensity that made her breathless. He had his head bowed, the blue glow of his eyes shining out from beneath his furrowed brow. He might have looked angry if she didn't know that... he was protecting her. Bolstering her through their connection. Whatever was going on within him, he wasn't rejecting her outright. At least, not yet.

Olivia cast a slight smile at him, then turned her attention back to the group she was trying to see as her patients. Three of them! Her smile broadened and came easier now that he had helped ease her pain. She gripped Lian's arms and gave her a little shake.

"Hey," Olivia said in a calm voice. "I am one-hundred percent happy for you. Okay?" Lian gave a brief nod. Olivia went on, smiling as big as she could. "You are not alone in this. Nancy and I are going to be the best Aunties in the world. In the universe. And we are going to spoil both of you rotten."

"Yeah?" Lian said.

"Yeah." Olivia pulled her into a hug, smiling at Nuar

He seemed to recover a bit. He was staring at Lian with an intensity that matched the look Bron had been giving Olivia a moment before. Whatever was in front of them, they would deal with it together. All of them. Olivia was sure that Lian and her baby would be fine. And Olivia... She would sort through her baggage on her own.

That cool breeze swept through her again, relaxing her muscles and soothing her aching heart. She looked over at Bron and smiled. He straightened, the intensity fading from his expression as he stopped doing whatever it was he had done to help her through this.

Maybe she wouldn't be as on her own as she thought.

Chapter Seven

The more time they spent together, the more Olivia's determination to understand whatever was standing between herself and Bron grew. Whether they could work it out... Well, she would deal with that when she had a better idea of what was going on. In the meantime, Lian and Nuar needed her.

"Lian told me that Cyan was here with you all," Olivia said.

The Vegan was an expert in xenobiology. To the little lizard person, humans and Cygnians were the aliens. They were beyond lucky to have her expertise, as well as access to her incredibly advanced technology.

"I'll go get her so she can conduct a more thorough evaluation," Bron said.

"Yes, yes, that's a great idea." Nuar still had a dazed look on his face as he stared at Lian.

"I'll go with you." Olivia released Lian to Nuar's eager embrace. She turned to find her own soulmate frowning at her. Did he not want her to come along? Well, too bad. She was going to figure out what his deal was. "These two could probably use a few minutes alone."

She breezed past Bron into the corridor, then turned back the way they had originally come. Bron fell in step behind her. Olivia straightened, keeping her head held high. She gave Zorro a little pat as they crossed through the room where the dogs were lounging and told them both to stay put. Once they were in the sizeable area with the hatch, she turned and stared at Bron expectantly. He stared back, his face slack and expressionless.

"You're going to have to touch me again to help me go..." She realized she didn't know where they were heading. "Wherever we're going."

"You don't have to accompany me," he said gruffly.

Olivia crossed her arms over her chest. "I'm not staying here by myself."

"You can stay with Lian."

"Lian and Nuar need some time alone to talk."

"Then you can stay with Tarn."

"No."

He did a bit of a double-take and a hint of unease crept into his features, the skin around his eyes tightening. She thought she almost felt a flutter of something from him, but the emotion vanished before she could figure out what it was.

"I don't know what it is about me that you're so afraid of," she only had suspicions, and she shoved those aside, "but you need to get over it so we can help Lian and

Nuar."

A flash of fire sparked to life in his eyes, their blue intensifying as they glowed. He took a deep breath, swelling his already massive chest to an even larger size. He didn't deny what she'd said. She had thought he would give her some speech about Cygnian warriors never being afraid. Lian had given Olivia the impression that these guys were always up for a fight, even amongst themselves. Maybe it was just her and Nuar or the Cygnians and each other. It was yet another sign that Bron hadn't accepted Olivia.

Bron stepped closer, towering over her. The heat in his eyes cooled as suddenly as if a shutter had closed within him. He struck his wristbands together and a moment after, the floor beneath her shifted, lowering toward the ground below the ship. A sharp wave of hurt swept through her, tightening her throat and making her stomach sour. She turned her back on him, not able to see that distant gaze any longer. Her own eyes blurred with tears that she did her best to blink away.

As the platform they stood on reached the ground, Bron said, "Olivia…"

"We're wasting time." She sniffed and wiped the moisture from her eyes. "If anyone can help Lian and her family, it's Cyan."

Olivia walked to the edge of the platform, a sense of unease growing within her. For the first time, she looked around at the desolate scene surrounding her. The *Arrow* was floating twenty feet above them, its milky white crystal radiating light that illuminated an enormous corridor carved from the rock of the dwarf planet they were within.

On their journey from Earth, Zemanni had told Olivia that the Tau Ceti had created a secret base in Ceres—the largest celestial body in the asteroid belt between Mars and Jupiter. When the Cygnians discovered it, along with the fact that the Tau Ceti in the base were trying to maneuver them into fighting at their side in their war with the Coalition of Planets, the Cygnian Queen had attacked, destroying what they thought was the entire facility.

Zemanni had remained suspicious, since the Cygnians had stayed at the site, as if guarding something. It turned out that the vast majority of the true facility was much deeper than they'd known. Materials that even the Vegans who were helping Bron and the other Cygnians couldn't analyze protected it.

As deep as they were, there was still evidence of the Cygnians' destruction all around them. The attack had dislodged huge chunks of rock from the asteroid's interior. They rotated in slow circles as they floated nearby in the zero-G environment. Gleaming bronze-colored metal flowed down a section of wall where it had melted and then cooled in a different shape. It was starkly beautiful, in an eerie, end-of-this-world sort of way.

Olivia shuddered, turning toward a large doorway marked with lights affixed to the cavern wall surrounding it. It wasn't far from the ship, but she didn't know where the shielding ran. She thought she saw a bit of a glimmer between them and the door, but wasn't sure. If the shield failed, it would expose her to both the cold vacuum of space and lethal amounts of radiation—not to mention taking away her oxygen and gravity.

Lian's stories included how the other Cygnians had immediately given their soulmates their own wristbands to protect them. If Nuar hadn't given her his wristbands, Lian would have died after being abducted. Bron had shown no sign that he was planning on giving Olivia his—or any—wristbands. She glared at him, trying to tamp down yet another hurt.

"Is it safe for me to head for the door?" she asked.

"The *Arrow* keeps a corridor active between the ship and the entrance to the base."

"Great."

She turned and started marching toward the door. As soon as they had sent Cyan to Lian, Olivia was going to have some choice words for Bron, along with a slew of questions. Did he have a death wish, rejecting her the way he seemed to be? Or maybe he thought if he kept her at arm's length, he could survive pushing her away. Did he not want a soulmate? Or did he just not want *her*?

Her chest felt like it was constricting. It wouldn't be the

first time she'd been cast aside because of what had happened to her. She had survived losing her fiancé. She would survive this. Only, it was so much more painful with Bron already. How could she care so much in such a short amount of time?

She tried to push away the doubts and focus on hope. That kiss in the corridor had been unbelievable. There *was* something between them. Something amazing and magical. Something worth fighting for.

Her thoughts were swirling, pulling her focus away from her surroundings. The door in front of her opened just as she reached it. A tiny green form darted out, running smack into her. Olivia instinctively reached out, hugging the little lizard person to her stomach so she wouldn't fall.

"Eep." Cyan blinked up at her with sparkling golden eyes, her pupils wide with excitement. The blue outlining her black stripes was brighter than usual and her scales were practically glowing emerald green against the silver bands of her exosuit. The scales on her cheeks were bright pink.

"Yikes, are you okay?" Olivia asked, feeling a flush come to her own cheeks. She had always wanted to hug Cyan, but the Vegans didn't seem that affectionate. To her surprise, Cyan hugged her back, her lips pulling into a huge smile.

"I am beyond okay," she said, excitement making her

voice rise to a high squeak. "Lian is having a baby. The first naturally conceived human-Cygnian hybrid. Beyond happiness for my friends in their good fortune and what this could mean for the future of both their people, this is an incredible opportunity to witness an epic alteration in their species' evolutionary paths."

Another Vegan came up behind her, the outlining of his black stripes a paler blue. He was shaking his head as he stared at Cyan, but the corners of his lips quirked up. He placed his hands on her shoulders, pulling her back from Olivia.

"And you can begin your studies sooner if we continue on our way," he said.

"Yes, yes, of course, Peri," Cyan said, in her sibilant voice. She pulled back from Olivia and folded her hands in front of her chest. Then, to Olivia's utter delight, the little Vegan started hopping up and down in place, her eyes crinkling almost shut from the huge smile on her face. "Lian is having a baby. Lian is having a baby!"

The tightness in Olivia's chest exploded out in a sob she could only half-cover, turning it into a laugh. She clamped her hand over her mouth and nodded, forcing herself back under control. Cyan's eyes softened. She stood still, cocking her head to the side as she stared at Olivia curiously. As soon as she could speak, Olivia dropped her hand, nodding even harder.

"Yes, she is, and she and that baby are going to need

you, so go on." Olivia waved toward the open hatch of the Arrow.

Peri took Cyan by her elbow and started steering her toward the ship. Cyan kept watching Olivia over her shoulder until they reached the platform. Peri squatted down, his tail whipping behind him, then he launched himself into the air, easily clearing the twenty feet to the ship. Cyan stared at Olivia for a moment longer, then followed.

Olivia took a deep, shuddering breath. She closed her eyes and let the tears flow for a moment, willing the pain to pass through her. Knowing it would. But each time, it seemed to leave her a little more hollow.

Cyan would help Lian. Maybe the Vegan could help Olivia as well. But maybe... Maybe she couldn't. Olivia loved to hold hope close to her heart always. She didn't know if she was strong enough to open herself to *this* hope. Not until she had figured things out with Bron.

"There is a deep pain within you." Bron's voice was low and even.

She turned to face him, letting him see the anguish on her features. If he felt what she felt, how could he be so calm?

Did he know? Did he even care? He ran so hot and cold. She wondered if she wanted to pursue being his soulmate. How could this be the other half of her soul?

From what Lian had said, Nuar was like a mirror in

some ways. She felt a wholeness after bonding with him fully, yet it wasn't as if either of them had been incomplete without the other. They complemented each other, strengthened each other. They worked because deep down, they were the same.

She studied Bron's expression for any sign that he could sense what she felt. That he shared it. All she saw was that blankness. That... shield. What was he hiding? What was *his* pain?

"I'm not the only one," she said.

Chapter Eight

Bron's chest was going to burst. The biogel surrounding his left heart was heating to unprecedented levels. His integrated circuitry was buzzing with both the static that had been plaguing him and now this new energy that Olivia was bringing forth. His nanites fed him a steady stream of alerts. Both his mechanical and biological components were suffering from a strain he'd never encountered.

It was nothing compared to the pain he had felt from within her. A pain he would do anything to ease.

"I need... I need to show you something," Bron said.

Olivia nodded, then turned and crossed through the still-open doorway to the secret base. His soulmate might be biological, but her soul was steel. Bron followed her, gesturing which way to turn when they had cleared the airlock. He stopped in front of the door to the main laboratory and office of Norem, the Tau Ceti scientist who had been in charge of the base. The one who had performed sadistic experiments on his own people and other life forms, grafting and manipulating DNA—and worse.

Norem had experimented on his own soldiers so that he could turn them into cyborgs. He had *dismembered* them.

A shudder wracked Bron as he remembered lying in a field of crystal, his blood staining the ground, and his father's terrified screams as he tried to piece Bron back together. Bron looked down, unable to hold Olivia's gaze as he fought back the memory. Rage and despair rose within him that someone would inflict that kind of harm on another for their own gain.

A red warning light flooded his vision, readouts scrolling through his view with dire messages about his systems. He couldn't afford to lose control. He also... He had to know what Olivia thought. What she might think of him if she ever found out what he had lost. Whether she could understand and accept what he had gained.

He didn't trust himself to move, so he dared to reach out to the base's computer systems through his internal communications network. The door slid open for them. He glanced up at Olivia to see her staring at him. Her brow was furrowed, and it was all he could do to keep himself from reaching up to smooth it.

"Please," he said, gesturing to the open door.

Olivia entered the room without a word. Bron followed, watching as she took everything in. Her brow tightened further as she passed a large caged-off area that had been used to house a dog that Norem had genetically engineered for reasons they hadn't determined yet. The only comfort the Cygnians and their soulmates had was that they knew the Tau Ceti on the base had held the animal in high regard and treated it well. If only Norem extended the same consideration to his own people.

Olivia barely glanced at the ornate wooden desk in the center of the room. Norem had developed a taste for Earth's opulent furnishings, as well as harvesting the planet's incredibly diverse DNA. But she had seen such things in her life, Bron was sure. What she hadn't seen was beyond the clear glass window that made up most of the wall in front of the desk.

Her eyes widened, and her mouth dropped open as she saw the holding tanks. They were huge—big enough to hold genetically altered Tau Ceti soldiers. Soldiers who Norem had turned into cyborgs without their consent. The three tanks ran from the floor to the ceiling, with flickering lights on control panels attached in various locations. Two were filled with a green-tinged fluid that did nothing to obscure her view of the life forms within.

Cyan was still trying to figure out what Norem had done to them. All she knew was that Norem had somehow grafted Cygnian and human DNA into their own Tau Ceti DNA—something that wasn't supposed to be possible at this stage of life. Genetic engineers usually only made such extensive alterations to embryos.

Bron shuddered at the thought of children being created

in such a way. Most sentients who propagated through genetic engineering kept their citizens in maturation chambers until they had a viable candidate. They left them there until they had reached adulthood, using Coalition mind programming tools to implant whatever skills and knowledge they wished the sentient to have when they emerged, fully grown and ready to 'contribute to society.' Except, their true purpose was to serve the High Council however those corrupt individuals desired. The thought sickened Bron.

Cygnians only reproduced naturally. It was one thing to assist someone by addressing any genetic issues that might cause them hardship in life. It was another to tailor each person to meet the needs of those in power.

Bron didn't want to think about what these Tau Ceti had experienced as Norem spliced and manipulated the DNA in every cell of their bodies. It was even harder to bear than seeing what he had done on a more obvious level.

Light gleamed off of the cybernetics that had replaced one of each of their arms and both legs. Bands of metal streaked up their torsos, strengthening their forms and integrating their augmentations more fully. They would be formidable opponents when they emerged. Or, more hopefully, formidable allies. But the personal cost...

Wires snaked in and out of their bodies, attached to devices floating near them. They didn't need any breathing apparatus. All Tau Ceti were amphibious and could extract oxygen and whatever other gasses they needed from the liquid surrounding them. Blinking diodes provided information that neither Bron nor Peri had sorted out yet. All they knew was that these two Tau Ceti-Cygnian hybrids had been an experiment that Norem intended to terminate.

A sadness swept through him, tempering Bron's own rage and bringing his attention back to the room. Back to his soulmate. Olivia had one hand clasped over her mouth and the other clutched her belly. She shook her head as tears rolled down her cheeks. Bron's hearts seemed to stop for a moment.

If only he could read her thoughts as easily as her emotions. A deep despair pervaded her feelings, tinged with fear and remorse. Olivia sniffed, pulling herself back under control. She dropped her hand from her mouth, but only to wrap both arms around her torso, as if hugging herself.

"What..." She coughed, but her voice still held a rasp when she went on. "What happened to them?"

"Norem."

"I don't understand. Were they... Were they in an accident?"

She paled a bit, swaying. Bron stepped closer in case she should collapse. If her reaction to the Tau Ceti soldiers was this powerful, how would she react when she learned of his own cybernetics?

"Lian didn't tell you of this?" Bron asked.

Olivia shook her head. "No. She wouldn't have—"

The door to the rest quarters attached to the office opened suddenly. Tobek stepped through, still pulling on the jacket of his uniform. Olivia stepped closer to Bron, her eyes widening as she took in the shining metal of his right arm before Tobek shrugged the jacket into place. His expression hardened, and he looked away.

Bron couldn't keep himself from imagining how it would feel for her to look at him that way. The surge of despair that rose in him was too powerful to control. Olivia turned to him, the caution clearly written on her features turning to concern.

"This is Tobek," Bron said. "He is… an ally."

Tobek let out a little snort of breath. "Really convincing. Since you're here to monitor the tanks, I'm going to go see how Lian is doing."

"She is with Cyan and Nuar," Bron said, an edge sharpening his words. "They don't need your help."

"Yeah, well, she calls me a friend instead of just an ally, so I'm going to make sure she knows that I'm around," Tobek retorted.

The others didn't need the distraction of an enhanced Tau Ceti soldier nearby. Lar's soulmate, Sophie, had sworn to them all that they could trust Tobek, but the mother of the first Cygnian-human offspring was at stake. Bron shifted his weight, intending to move to block Tobek as he headed for the door. Olivia reached out and grasped Bron's hand, interlacing their fingers. He sucked in a breath as a wave of calmness washed through him.

"She mentioned you," Olivia said with a big smile. "I think she'd really like that."

Tobek stared at Olivia for a moment before his face softened into a smile. He nodded, then headed for the door, murmuring a quiet, "Thanks," as he passed them. When the door closed behind him and they were alone, she turned back to Bron.

"Lian trusts Tobek," Olivia said. "Seeing him will make her feel better."

Bron couldn't suppress a low growl. Most of the others had accepted Tobek as one of their own. Bron was still adjusting to the idea of being able to trust a Tau Ceti, even if they held Cygnian DNA.

Or maybe I'm jealous that he is free to share who he is with anyone he wants.

Bron tried to shove the thought away. He should be grateful for his second chance. He *was* grateful for it. But having to keep who and what he was a secret, having to suppress his abilities and hide what he could do his entire life, had worn on him.

"They have spent time together. Tobek was stationed on Earth for several years as a scout before..." Bron's voice trailed off as he glanced at the tanks.

Olivia followed his line of sight. A shiver coursed through her and she tightened her grip on his hand—his right hand.

"Was he in the empty one?" Olivia asked.

"Perhaps."

She shook her head. "They match."

"What do you mean?"

"The same limbs have been replaced. It doesn't look accidental. It looks premeditated."

"It was. Norem is the Tau Ceti scientist who ran this base. He fled before we could capture him."

"Lian didn't give me many details. She just said that the guy in charge of the place where she was almost taken had been abducting people and that you're still trying to find someone he took. She always seemed to leave things out. When she talked about you trying to figure out the technology he left behind, I didn't know anything like this would be involved."

"It troubles you that they are so much machine." The words came out flat, a dull ache suffusing his chest.

"No, it troubles me that they had to endure so much pain."

"They're stronger for it. They will be faster than the other Tau Ceti soldiers and have special abilities."

"But did they ask for it?" She turned to stare at Bron. "Did they ask for any of it?"

Bron's jaw ached from how hard he clenched his teeth.

If she knew what he had endured, would she see pain every time she looked at him? He shook his head, unable to bear the thought. He tried to shutter the emotion, but having her near was making those emotions stronger, destroying the tenuous control he could usually manage.

Bron's voice was gruff when he spoke. "From what Tobek said, some volunteered. Most didn't."

"Who could do something like this to anyone?"

"Sometimes, there isn't a choice."

She glanced up at him just as his cybernetics let out an intense burst of static. Pain seared along his nerves and his hearts beat frantically. His left side spasmed, his leg buckled and dropped him to one knee. Olivia tried to slow his descent, following him to the ground and kneeling in front of him. She rested one hand on the back of his neck as he pinched his eyes shut, willing his body to come back under his control.

"Breathe," she said. "Breathe with me."

She started taking loud, deep breaths. He did his best to follow them. His hearts calmed, coming closer to matching her steady beat. Gradually, the pain passed, the static lessening. At this rate, she wouldn't see a remembrance of pain when she looked at him. She'd be seeing it in real-time. The episodes were becoming more frequent and intense.

"What do you need me to do?" she asked, her voice strong and calm.

'Accept me for who I am?' he thought.

But hadn't she already said that she did? Bron opened his eyes to see her staring intently into his. Their faces were close enough to feel each other's warm breath. He could sense her desire to help, to understand him and become closer. To bond. His chest felt overfull, energy passing between them as their souls sought a deeper connection, sought unity.

Was sharing his secret with her divulging it to another? Olivia held the other half of his soul. She was already a part of him and deserved to know... everything.

He gently clasped her wrist, daring to touch her with his left hand. She didn't flinch or eye it strangely. Her heart quickened its pace, her lips parting. He realized he was leaning closer, but stopped himself. Before anything more happened between them, she needed to know.

"I need to show you something," he repeated.

Chapter Nine

Olivia followed Bron through the door that Tobek had entered from. The room on the other side was a spacious dorm. Several beds lined the polished brass walls, and there were two bushes with thick, slanted branches that made her wonder if the Vegans bunked here as well. Bron led Olivia to a bed and turned her, urging her to sit, though he remained standing.

When the silence stretched on for several minutes, she said, "You wanted to show me something?"

He backed up a few paces, his features vacillating between that odd slack look and one that matched the feeling of torn desperation emanating from him in bursts, almost like a strobe light. His eyes pinched at the corners, and she could feel his hearts pounding, her own being pulled along with his erratic beats.

This was nothing at all like what Lian had described, aside from the fact that Olivia could feel what Bron felt—when there wasn't that wall between them. She sensed the bond connecting them, and his shared desire to explore it —along with something else. An echo of her own fear of rejection? Or was it his own?

"I think we both have some... concerns about how things might proceed between us," she said, keeping her voice light. "So, why don't I go first?"

His intensity was palpable, his eyes gleaming bright blue as he stared at her. She noticed she was wringing her hands in her lap and forced them apart, placing them flat on her thighs. She wanted to get this over with. If it ended things between them before they really began, so be it. She would rather have that than give away years of her life only to be dumped after—

She shook her head harshly, pushing away the memories. This was about looking ahead. Lian said that soulmate bonds were the universe bringing together two people who were perfect for each other, even if it took them a while to see it. If that was the case, surely Bron would understand and accept her, just as she was. The way she wanted to understand and accept him.

"I can't have children," she said. Her voice was calm, though her throat had tightened and her eyes burned.

His eyes narrowed. "What do you mean?"

"I was in an accident. My fiancé was driving and—" She stopped herself, shaking her head again, and looked down at the floor. "Well, that doesn't matter. What matters is that I was injured. Severely. I was in the hospital for months, and after..." She swallowed hard. "The damage and scarring are extensive. I don't know if even the Vegans can help me. So, if that's a problem—"

Her voice cut off as she looked up to see Bron's eyes glowing with an intense blue light. Even through his beard, she could see a muscle working in his jaw. Despair rolled off of him as clearly as if he were ranting about his disappointment in her. Olivia wasn't about to sit there and take it. She stood and headed for the door. Just before she reached it, Bron spoke again.

"You have a bondmate already," he said.

She stopped, her back to him, and closed her eyes. Her heart was pounding so hard her ribs hurt, and her throat was almost too tight to breathe. How much disappointment of her own could she take before her heart broke permanently? She tried to keep it open to others, to the goodness in the world. Except she had been betrayed so harshly already. To think that the universe might dangle her soulmate in front of her, only to yank him away…

No. The universe wasn't like that. She refused to believe it.

"I apologize," Bron said. "I didn't know when I… When I kissed you."

She let out a disgusted snort, then turned around. "When *we* kissed. I kissed you back." She lifted an arm briefly before letting it drop to her side. Slowly, she walked closer to him once more. Olivia stopped right in front of him, determined to see this through.

"I was once engaged to have a bondmate," she said.

"But when he found out I couldn't have children, he left me." She looked away, fighting the coldness that always entered her heart when she thought about watching him leave while she laid there, wires and tubes hooked up to her body much the same as the cyborgs in the other room. She hugged herself when she shuddered. "I wasn't even close to being discharged from the hospital. It took months before I was well enough to leave. I guess he couldn't or wouldn't wait to move on with his life with someone who could give him a family."

A greater cold swept through her, along with a white-hot rage. She gasped from the intensity of it and studied Bron's expression for any clues about what he was thinking. He had clenched his hands into fists so tight, the blue of his skin paled. The air behind him shimmered from the vibration of his spine plates, which must be standing straight up. His eyes blazed beneath his lowered brow.

Through teeth so tight, she wondered how he spoke, he said, "Does he still live?"

Another wave of fury—murderous fury—rolled out of him. If her ex-fiancé were in the room, she knew Bron would crush him. But she didn't want that. She wanted to move on and leave the past behind her. She stepped forward and clasped Bron's wrist. He flinched, but didn't recoil. Instead, he stood absolutely still, barely even breathing.

"I'm not the kind of person who dwells in the past,"

Olivia said. "It was a horrible thing that happened, and now it's behind me. I've moved on with my life and will continue to do so. And... I want to explore us and what this soulmate bond means. I want to move forward with *you.*"

Bron's arm vibrated beneath her touch, then jerked suddenly as if he was having a muscle spasm. He pulled away from her, grabbing his arm and holding it braced against his side. As he stepped back, his left leg buckled, taking him down to one knee again. She lowered herself with him, her hands on his shoulders, as if she could keep the massive Cygnian upright on her own. Why did this keep happening to him?

"Oh my god, Bron, what's wrong?" She turned toward the door, sucking in a breath to cry for help, but Bron grabbed her right hand with his, squeezing it against his shoulder.

"Don't," he said. "Please."

"You need help."

"They can't help me. No one can."

Anger and frustration rose in her. "Now, you listen to me. If you think you're the only one of us who can be stubborn, you're fooling yourself. That's a trait we share, not one we diminish in the other. There is no way I'm going to sit here and watch you suffer."

He closed his eyes and lowered his head, shaking it. Olivia lifted her free hand to his face, urging him to look at her again. When he did, she went on in a gentler tone.

"I am your soulmate," she said. "I don't know what that means to you, but for me, it means that we face everything together. I'm here to help you carry your burdens, as I expect you to help me carry mine. We have to be there for each other and accept each other as we are. That's what this means to me. But if you can't open your heart to me, then we never stood a chance. If we are soulmates and you can't trust me, that means you can't trust yourself."

"I want to trust you, Olivia."

The longing in his voice wound through her heart, quickening its beat. She dared to lean forward and brush her lips against his. He returned the kiss, deepening the contact. He released her hand from his shoulder, grasping her waist as he rose to his feet, bringing her with him. His hands slid down to her backside, lighting a fire in her core that sent heat thrumming through her. Instead of lifting her from the ground, he broke off the kiss and stepped back, shaking his head. He turned and walked away, one hand propped on his hip and the other running through his dark hair.

"You are part of me," he said. "Because of that... Because of that, sharing this will not break my oath."

What oath? Lian had told Olivia about a vow Lar had taken that had kept him from bonding with his soulmate and nearly—actually, for a time—taken his life. Had Bron sworn something similar?

He gestured toward the bed she had risen from and said, "Sit. Please."

"I'm fine standing."

Bron hesitated a few moments, then said, "When you saw the soldiers in the tanks, you had a powerful reaction."

"I did. It... It reminded me of when I was hospitalized and hooked up to machines and bags of fluids and—" She shook her head sharply. She needed not to think about that. If those men in the other room needed her, she wanted to be calm enough to help them.

"There was more," Bron said. "Beyond that."

"Yes. I hate to think of how much pain they've gone through to be as they are."

"Do you think you can ever see beyond it?"

"I don't understand why you're asking this."

"Please, I need to know what you think of the cyborgs."

She could feel how important this was to Bron, even if she didn't know why. She thought about it for a few moments.

"I feel terrible about what happened to them. I'm mad that someone looked at them and didn't think that they were enough as they were. Putting someone through that on purpose is despicable."

"What if it had been necessary?" Bron asked.

"Was it?"

He looked away, disappointment and despair flowing out from him. "The sight of them will always bring you thoughts of their pain and yours."

"No, it won't. I didn't feel bad for Tobek when I saw him. He's on the other side of it. I still feel sympathy for what he's been through, but it's not so... visceral."

A spark of hope crept through Bron's emotions. Hope mixed with dread.

"Bron, come on," she said. "I believed in soulmates before your people even came to Earth. Before I saw with my own eyes how perfect Lian and Nuar are for each other. I believe in us enough that I followed you halfway across our solar system when I've never been outside of Kansas before. Whatever it is, I can handle it."

His eyes were wide, his lips parted as he stared at her. He snapped his mouth shut, his brow furrowing in determination as he stepped back. He lifted his hands in front of his torso, pausing at the ties for the white leather tunic he wore. Then he began loosening the laces. He pulled the garment over his head and tossed it aside. The light gleamed across the deep blue of his skin, rippling over enormous biceps and a chest bulging with defined muscle. His abs stood out in sharp rows, well more than a six-pack. His waist was still narrow, compared to the rest of him, but perfectly in proportion.

The vibration of his spine plates intensified. The hum they sent through the air resonated in her as tingling pleasure flowed through her nerves, pooling low in her belly. He undid the fastener of his pants and Olivia's mouth went dry. She knew what to expect, thanks to Lian's stories. Bron kicked off his boots, then pushed his pants down to the ground, stepping out of them.

Two massive blue dicks hung from his groin, stacked one on top of the other. Just looking at them made Olivia's nipples harden and her core tighten with need. She had no idea how she was going to manage him, but was eager to try. Her mind fogged with lust. Hadn't there been a purpose to this? Something Bron was trying to tell her? If he thought anything about himself wasn't perfect, she wasn't seeing it.

Their gazes met and locked, the bright blue light of his irises almost too intense to hold. He struck his wristbands together, his deep voice humming in his chest. The command note caused his wristbands to expand until he could slide them from his wrists. He stepped closer, and she nearly ran to him, her need to be closer consuming all thought. Instead of taking her in his arms, he held out the wristbands in offering.

She smiled, lifting her hands so that he could slide the gleaming chrome-colored crystal onto her wrists. Another hummed note had her writhing, his voice resonating within her in all the right places. The wristbands tightened to fit her perfectly. Bron's hands lingered, still clasping the devices. Fear overwhelmed his own desire. What could he be afraid of?

"I accept you," she whispered, the words leaving her lips without thought. "Whatever burdens you carry, I will carry them with you."

A shuddering breath escaped him and he lowered his head, then shook it. "I am the luckiest Cygnian who has ever lived. To have a soulmate such as you. And…"

When the silence dragged on, she gently prompted, "And?"

"And to have been saved."

"Saved?" What could a Cygnian need to be saved from? They were nearly indestructible.

Bron lifted her hands to his lips, pressing a kiss to her knuckles, then he stepped back and dropped his grip on her wristbands.

Shimmering light spread over the left side of his body. His blue skin brightened to a gleaming chrome on his left arm and leg, as well as a significant portion of that side of his torso. The revealed metal crept over his chest, forming one of his pectoral muscles, and veered up across his abdomen in two sharp triangles that tapered to points as they neared his right side. The places where metal met flesh were so integrated, she couldn't tell where one stopped and the other began. Aside from the color and the flat, segmented lines that adorned the chrome, both sides of his body looked natural, unlike the somewhat bulkier metal parts of the men in the tanks.

This wasn't premeditated. She was certain of that. But what had happened to him? What could have done this to a Cygnian warrior? He lifted his head so he could study her eyes, and the stark vulnerability she saw there tugged at her pounding heart.

It didn't matter what was in the past. He needed her, now. Needed her understanding and compassion. She would give it to him.

Chapter Ten

Bron couldn't breathe. His hearts stuttered, their mismatched beats becoming even more out of sync as he waited for Olivia to say or do something, anything. Her soft eyes had widened and her lush lips were parted. He tried to keep his emotions from her, but knew they were too strong. And as long as he kept himself shielded from her, he couldn't clearly tell what she was feeling.

She took a step closer, then another. With a shaking hand, she reached out and rested her palm on the left side of his body, splaying her fingers over the metal of his chest. The heart beneath it stuttered, then pounded harder, as if trying to reach her through the biogel and cabling surrounding it.

"Bron..." she said, her voice trembling.

"It causes me no pain."

That had been such a concern to her. He wanted to reassure her. Unfortunately, as if to contradict his words, his left leg spasmed again, excruciating static spreading to his left arm and making it jerk.

"That was pain," she said.

"It will pass."

He closed his eyes and took deep breaths, willing his body back under control. The nanites within him rushed to stabilize the various systems that were malfunctioning. Gradually, the static subsided.

"I'll go get Peri," she said. "Or Tarn."

He caught her hand as she pulled away, keeping it pressed against his chest. "They can't help me."

"Well… Maybe Cyan." A tear slid down her cheek and she sniffed. Bron reached out with his free hand and wiped it away. "Surely someone can at least help you with the pain you're in. Someone should know what to do."

"They don't even know about this. About me."

"What?" Her delicate brow furrowed. "Why not?"

"Because the aliens who saved me are one of the most reclusive species in the universe. They swore my family and myself to secrecy, as well as Queen Ehmach, who arranged it all."

"Arranged for you to have to suffer in silence?" Olivia's anger warmed him. He pulled her closer.

"She arranged for me to be saved." Bron shook his head, a renewed sense of wonder and gratitude making his chest feel full. "I begged my father to take me on a hunting trip with him and my brother, Dorn, even though I wasn't of age. My tissues hadn't strengthened yet, leaving me vulnerable. They thought they could keep me from the beryl beast they hunted, but it escaped their control and targeted me."

A shudder passed through him that had nothing to do with his system malfunctions. He could still see the beast as clearly as if it was in the room with him, the intense light of the crystal shielding above Cygnus-prime's sky washing out the deep blue of its pelt. The warriors in their party had thought it was stunned, but it was larger than most—as big as many of the houses Bron had seen in Harbor. It rallied from the insufficient charges in their weaponry and lashed out, targeting Bron as the smallest and weakest of the group.

His ears still rang with the warriors' shouts as they tried to pull the thing off of him. He could still feel it pawing at him, shredding his body against the hard terrain of the Cygnian plains, his blood flowing into blades of crystalline grass.

"Bron..." Olivia's gentle whisper brought him back to himself and the room surrounding them.

"Ehmach stood above me and asked if I wanted to live. I said yes, and she told me I would have to fight for it. She had me placed on her personal fighter and flew me to the planet where I was... rebuilt."

"Healed." Olivia stepped closer, clasping his hands in hers and holding them up between their chests. "Where you were healed."

Bron nodded. His hearts felt as if they were being squeezed within his chest, as if there wasn't room to accommodate them. Olivia's acceptance and understanding infiltrated through his being, soothing the pain that had plagued both his mind and his body.

"I still don't understand why Tarn and Peri can't help you," Olivia said. "They don't have to know where your cybernetics came from."

"They'll know. As much as people believe the Vegans have the most advanced technology in the galaxy, there are others who rival or even surpass them in certain areas. The sentients who helped me know more about cybernetics than any other civilization. If an engineer examines me for more than a few moments, they will see that my systems are well beyond the currently existent civilizations' technology. Then they'll start thinking of legends, and eventually, they will come upon the Psiarae."

A wave of bitterness edged into the gratitude he had felt a moment before. Olivia angled her head to the side, her eyes narrowing.

"What was that?" she asked.

"Something shameful." He shook his head. "I should be nothing but grateful for being saved. I only wish…"

He looked away, but she released his hands and reached up to wrap her arms around his shoulders, rising on her tip-toes as if that could bring them face-to-face. He clasped his arms around her, pressing her tight and bending lower.

"What do you wish?" she said. "You can tell me

anything."

He nodded, then let out a long breath. "I wish they had made me with less advanced technology."

"So you wouldn't have to hide what you are from others?"

"So I wouldn't have to hide what I can do. The others in my prism wouldn't have any issues with me being a cyborg. But if they knew what my enhancements enable me to do..." He shook his head.

"They would still accept you," she said.

"Perhaps. Or they would view my secrets as a betrayal. They would question every victory I'd ever had with them, wondering if it was my enhanced abilities and not my Cygnian nature that had won in the end."

"I don't understand."

"The Psiarae aren't just the most adept at merging biological and mechanical systems. They infused me with ultra-advanced nanites. They built in functionality that outstrips any technology I've ever encountered. The others think I'm excellent with computers and can hack through any system. But it isn't because of my knowledge and skill. It's my very makeup that allows me to do so. I could command the *Arrow* by myself. I can access the ship's databases, communications arrays, medical scanners, everything—with just a thought."

"You think they'll be jealous?"

"I think they might feel obsolete. Or worse, they might

give over all of those functions to me, as if I'm just another of the ship's systems."

"Bron…" She tightened her grip on his shoulders, pulling herself closer. "This is your prism. Your warrior-brothers. Will they give you crap about this?" She angled her head and smiled. "Probably. But they won't reject you. And if they try to take advantage of you, we'll kick their asses. Anyway, you're going to have plenty of other things to occupy your thoughts."

"Like isolating my system errors?"

"That." Her smile deepened. "And this."

She pulled him down to her, pressing her lips to his. Pleasure arced through him, racing along nerve-endings both biological and constructed. The static vanished as her heat and proximity overwhelmed everything else. His hearts pounded, their beats growing closer to unity. Bron let his hands slide down to cup her ass, lifting her from her feet once more so she could wrap her legs around his waist. His skin and dermal sensors tingled with awareness everywhere they touched. The surrounding air shimmered from the intense vibration of his spine plates. His dicks hardened, their crowns jutting against her, prodding the molten heat of her core.

Bron deepened the kiss, caressing her lips with his, running his tongue across the seam of her mouth. She opened to him and he plunged within, but kept his strokes gentle. She let out a frustrated grunt, tightening her grip on his neck and running one hand through his hair, scraping her nails across his scalp. He growled in response, sensing her need for his passion. She broke off the kiss and pulled back enough to stare into his eyes.

"You better activate those shields in these wristbands," she said. "Because I want everything you can give me. No more holding back."

Bron nodded, then walked her to the bed he used in the rest area. He pulled her legs away from his waist so that she could stand on the foot of the bed. Olivia smiled as she looked at him from the same height he stared at her from when they stood on the same level. She leaned in and kissed him, running her fingers through his hair again, every touch sending waves of pleasure through him. She was right about the shields. He needed to ensure her safety as quickly as possible.

Running his hands over the fabric of her dress, he found the zipper that held it together and drew it down. He shifted back just enough to let the garment fall to her ankles, then reached down and tossed it aside. He broke off their kiss, his lips exploring her sepia skin, his hands lifting her breasts. She gasped as he ran his thumb across the tight bud of her nipple, clutching his head tighter when he dropped his mouth to it. Hooking his fingers in the waistband of her panties, he slid the pale yellow fabric down her legs, casting them away as well.

He dropped to his knees, gripping her hips to pull her

closer. He lifted one of her legs over his shoulder and used one arm to hold her up. A tremor passed through his left side, reminding him he needed to hurry.

Whenever he had hummed command notes for his wristbands, he had felt Olivia's response through their bond. This time, he wanted to feel it through their bodies.

He pressed his lips to the soft curls between her legs, lapping at her clit. She gasped again, her fingers tightening in his hair. Bron began the command sequence to activate shielding that would keep her safe should he use too much pressure or strength, while also letting her feel everything he did to her. Her breath caught, then she moaned, her body seeming to match the vibration of his low voice. His spine plates added their own resonance to it, rippling through his body and into her.

"Oh..." She gasped when he deepened the pressure, pulling her clit between his lips.

The shields were active, but her reaction was too intoxicating for Bron to stop. He went through diagnostic routines, scanning functions, anything that wouldn't interfere with her safety, while also drawing out the pleasure she took from feeling him hum against this most intimate spot of her body.

He drew his fingers along her slit, gathering her wetness, then thrust two deep within her. She was so tight. He massaged her, spreading his fingers to help prepare her body for their bonding, increasing the speed of his movements within her and the intensity of the pressure without. Her body stiffened, then her hips bucked against him, her grip on his head tightening as her core throbbed around his fingers. He didn't let up, coaxing every ounce of pleasure from her that he could. Only when he felt her hands grow lax did he stop.

He kept his grip on her as he knelt on the bed's edge, then half-crawled further up onto its surface, carrying Olivia with him. Thank the Maker they had all taken to sleeping on soft beds, hoping to be more prepared for the day they found their own Earthling soulmates. She sank into the cushioned surface, her brown eyes smoldering as she stared up at him. His soulmate. His everything.

Chapter Eleven

Olivia couldn't believe how much she still wanted Bron after the mind-shattering orgasm he'd just given her. But as he hovered above her, propped on his elbows, she couldn't wait to feel him inside of her again. To feel all of him. Her spine was a constant current of energy, the electric arcs flowing out from it, heightening every touch.

Bron lowered himself on top of her, claiming her lips in a deep, possessive kiss. One of his erections nudged at her entrance. She drew her legs up along his thighs, encouraging him. He seemed ready to take his time here as well, but she was near desperate with need. She'd never wanted anyone like this before. Her entire body cried out for him, her cells alive as they'd never been.

"Bron, please," she pleaded.

He let out a rumbling growl of approval, the vibration of his voice passing through his chest and into her, setting her off again. She wrapped her thighs around his and pulled, trying to draw him closer. With maddening care, he shifted his hips forward, his lower dick parting the hot folds of her flesh while the upper slid along her clitoris. The sensations were almost too intense to bear.

"Bron," she repeated, this time digging her fingertips into the flesh of his ass. Trying to, anyway. If it weren't for the shields protecting her, she would have broken a nail.

With a swift movement, he plunged into her, stretching her, filling her, heightening that intense energy coursing through her until her awareness narrowed to just the spot where they were joined. He paused for a few moments as her body adjusted to him, then started to move. Again, with the slow, languid movements that let her feel every inch of him as he slid from her body, then thrust deep.

He shifted his weight to his left arm, then reached between them and cupped her breast, flicking his thumb across her nipple. She gasped, arching into his touch. His kisses trailed along her jaw to her neck, where he sucked on her skin and ran his sharp teeth over its surface. The movement of his hips against hers was almost hypnotic, but she could feel him holding himself back.

She pushed against him and said, "Roll over."

He froze, further evidence that he wasn't really letting himself go. But then he rolled to the side, pulling her with him. She straddled him, supporting herself with her hands against his chest as she took a moment to adjust to the new angle. Shifting her weight onto her knees, she drew herself up along his length, moaning as pleasure tore along her nerves. As she settled back onto him, she lifted herself upright, taking him as deep as she could.

Bron's hands clenched on her hips, his jaw taut beneath

the dark hair of his beard. His eyes glowed like beacons, the intensity of his stare sending a thrill through her. What would it take for him to lose control?

She rose on her knees again, twisting her hips as she did in a corkscrew movement. His eyes widened and he pressed his head against the pillows. Better. She sank back down, a shiver of delight coursing through her spine as he hissed out a breath. His hips shifted up, lifting her higher, as if he was trying to get even deeper. She grasped his wrists as she kept up her movements and lifted his hands to her breasts, using them to fondle her nipples and encouraging him to take over kneading them.

That focused look was inching back into his eyes. She understood he had needed to be controlled before. He had to keep his secret from the others. But with her, she wanted him to be completely free. She wanted to break through the walls he'd built around himself. It was the only way he'd ever truly feel safe with her.

"Trust yourself, Bron," she said. "Trust yourself the same way I trust you."

His lips parted slightly, and the lines of concentration around his eyes lessened. He sat up so that his chest was against hers, wrapping his arms around her and drawing her down for a kiss. His tongue slid between her lips— gentle at first, but then more demanding. His hands gripped her hips, lifting her higher along his length, then pulling her down while angling his hips to deepen each thrust.

Pleasure flooded through her, coiling deep in her belly. With their bodies pressed together, his other dick rubbed against her clit, bringing her closer to the edge. She reached between them and grasped it, squeezing it as she gave it a long stroke, determined to take him with her to the edge of bliss. His breath rushed out of him with a groan. He quickened his pace, his hands tightening on her hips as she crashed down on him again and again, all the while keeping her hand wrapped around his upper shaft, her core clutching his lower one.

He let out a loud roar, then flipped her over onto her back, his arms beneath her and his hands clutching her shoulders. She gripped his hips as he bucked against her wildly, his thrusts almost frenzied. The pleasure he had so carefully stoked within her broke free in an explosion of ecstasy that dimmed her vision. Her body was thrumming with it when she came back to herself, but Bron was still going.

He held her in place with his arms, pounding into her. He slowed for only a moment, pulling himself from her, then lining up his other dick and thrusting deep, filling her even more fully than before. A gasping growl escaped him as he kept up his movements, one hand sliding down to lift her thigh and wrap her leg around his waist. She lifted the other herself, clasping her ankles behind his back to let him land deeper.

His huge hand kept its hold on her leg as his lips found hers again. His tongue plunged into her mouth, conquering and pleading, as if he was starving for her. She met him with everything she had, arching her hips against his, raking her nails along his back, devouring him. Somehow, even after all the pleasure he'd given her, she was still hungry for more. She would always want more of him, more of this.

His dick pulled against her core with each thrust, the incredible friction sending spirals of pleasure through her. Her bones vibrated with it, her body saturated with him. The energy coiled within her again, deeper than before, resonating in every cell, then exploded out in a burst that blinded her with light instead of dimming her vision. She cried out his name as a shockwave pulsed out from his body, vibrating through her, through the bed and even the walls. His dick pulsed as he buried himself as deep as he could, letting out another guttural cry as he spilled his seed within her.

They held each other, their panting breath the loudest thing in the room. A heady mix of awe and peace radiated from Bron. She felt it reflecting in her own heart, the love and hope she already felt for him, for their future, adding to it. Rainbows floated in the air all around, a beautiful byproduct of their achieving unity. Bron nuzzled her neck, then pressed a much more gentle kiss to her lips.

When he pulled back, she grinned and said, "See? I

told you I could handle it."

His lips pulled into a smile—the first true smile she had seen from him—and it took her breath away. "I will never doubt you again."

Her core tightened around him and he groaned, his hips rocking against hers seemingly of their own accord.

"So, that's unity," she said.

He nodded. "That is unity. We are forever bonded now. We are one."

Olivia's smile broadened enough to make her cheeks hurt. She was so happy. "That's great and all, but…"

"But?" He arched an eyebrow, obviously picking up on the playful emotions coursing through her.

"When can we do it again?"

He laughed, then ran a hand along her side to her thigh. "Whenever you wish."

"Hmm, I like the sound of that."

The lights flickered and an odd mechanical hum started behind the paneling of the room, as if something was powering up.

"I do *not* like the sound of that," she said.

"Nor do I."

Bron rolled to his side and rose on one elbow, looking around the room as if seeking the source of the sound. His eyes widened, and he leapt up from the bed.

"Dress," he said. "Quickly."

"What is it?" Olivia jumped up as she spoke and ran

for her dress, pulling it up over her body and reaching behind her for the zipper. Bron had his pants on and was already headed for the door by the time she was done.

"Bron," she repeated. "What's going on?"

"It's the cyborgs," he said. "They're awakening."

Chapter Twelve

Alert klaxons shrieked through the air as Bron tore into the room containing the tanks with the two hybrid cyborgs. Beneath the piercing noise, he felt more than heard a pulse indicating someone was trying to communicate with them. Olivia had his wristbands, and there was no way he was taking them back from her when he didn't know how this situation was going to play out. There was no time to show her how to activate the comm channel. Instead, Bron sent out a mental command that shut off the alarms and opened the communication channel in the room using his nanites.

"We're on our way," Tobek yelled. "What's going on?"

"One of the cyborgs is emerging from his tank," Bron said.

The farthest tank from the door to the rest chamber was draining. Bron ran to it, ready to assist the soldier within. The man's eyes were wide open, his pupils huge with fear. Three gills on each side of his neck pulsed open and closed as he took the equivalent of fast breaths. The wires connected to various parts of his body suddenly detached and the tank pulled up into the ceiling. He collapsed into Bron's arms, choking and gasping as he expelled the tank's liquid from his lungs so that he could switch to breathing air.

"Breathe, brother," Bron said, lowering him to the floor. "I've got you."

A wave of panic hit him just before Olivia cried out, "Bron!"

Both men turned to see her plastered against the third tank, her fingers hooked beneath one of the control panels as she pulled with all her might. Was she trying to lift it? Bron looked within the tank and his hearts nearly stopped. The soldier within was awake, his eyes wide and his body jerking in uncontrolled spasms. The liquid near him lit up as the wires that had detached from him sparked, arcing through his body.

"Alek!" The man he had helped tried to rise, but Bron pushed him back.

Bron ran across the room, interfacing with the computers as he did. The sensors had malfunctioned and thought this subject's tank had drained. Bron tried to override the system's commands, ordering it to open the tank, but the lifting mechanism was jammed.

"We have to do something." Olivia grunted as she gripped the side of the tank from a different angle and tried again to move it.

Bron accessed the commands of her wristbands, activating every type of shielding he could think of. She jerked back in surprise, staring at her arms as a thin layer of golden light spread over her skin. The shields would protect her from every kind of contaminant, environmental hazard, or energy pulse to their utmost abilities. Bron still had no idea what was in the slurry of fluids that held Norem's 'experiments,' and he didn't want so much as a drop to touch her skin.

"Go help the other one," he said.

She opened her lips as if to argue, but then snapped her mouth shut and nodded. As quickly as she could, she ran to the other side of the chamber and started helping the cyborg to crawl farther away. Bron said a silent prayer to the Maker, then pulled his arm back and struck the tank as hard as he could. Cracks spread through the transparent material from the impact site. Bron hit it again and again, watching as the man within—Alek—kept jerking in pain as the tank electrocuted him. His eyelids drooped.

"Fight, Alek," Bron shouted, slamming his fist into the tank again. "Fight for your life. Whatever you were before, you're a Cygnian warrior now. Cygnians fight. So fight!"

With a final blow, the material shattered. The greenish-yellow liquid within spewed out, running down Bron's torso and legs, drenching him. He didn't care. He reached in through the hole he'd created as the tank's fluid poured over him. Clenching his teeth, he grabbed the wires and yanked them from the conduits in the top of the tank. Electricity arced through him, setting his nerves on fire. The pain was nothing compared to the static he'd been experiencing the last few days. The shocks stopped as the cables came free from their housings.

He caught Alek as he fell forward, trying to keep him from the jagged shards surrounding the hole Bron had created. Sibilant hissing sounded behind him. He craned his neck over his shoulder to see Peri and Cyan standing in the doorway, their golden eyes huge with shock as they stared at him. They were speaking in a language he couldn't understand. Their tone clearly conveyed their astonishment.

Tobek pushed his way past them, rushing to Bron's side, then lifted his right arm with his hand fisted. A beam of intense yellow light emerged from the top of his cybernetic wrist. Tobek carefully used the laser to cut away at the tank, first removing the jagged edges Bron had made, then enlarging the hole.

The Vegans seemed to have recovered from their initial shock and now stood at their side. They lifted their hands, fingers splayed wide as they used the artificial gravity controls of their exosuits to help maneuver Alek safely from the tank. The other cyborg had recovered enough to join them, pulling Alek's arm over his shoulder to help him stand.

"Merek," Alek blearily said.

"I've got you." Merek looked up at Bron and nodded. *"We've* got you."

Warmth flowed through him. Olivia's love and

understanding had awakened so much within him. He could accept these men. He *would* accept them. Whatever they had started as, they were Cygnians now—and cyborgs, just as he was himself. The warmth grew, suffusing his biological components, rippling across his skin. As Bron breathed, the air in the room burned his heated lungs.

This wasn't right.

"Bron?" Olivia gripped his arm tight, her eyes wide with worry.

"I'm all right," Bron said, just as the room tilted in his perception, as if the gravity regulators were malfunctioning. He tried to lift his left arm to brush her hair away from her face, but it just hung at his side, the weight of its metal more noticeable than usual.

"You are not all right." She placed her hand on his forehead. "You're burning up. What was in those tanks?"

"We don't know," Tobek said, standing closer. His stance conveyed a readiness for action.

"We are still analyzing its contents," Cyan said. "There are aspects of Norem's formula that elude us, but the liquid shouldn't be able to permeate a Cygnian's skin."

"What about his cybernetics?" Olivia asked.

Peri shook his head. "Even the most rudimentary cybernetics are 'waterproofed,' as you Earthlings would say. And this…" Peri angled his head and peered closely at Bron's chest. "This is far from rudimentary."

He jerked back, a frill around his neck and cheeks expanding. Bron hadn't known Vegans had such physical attributes. Peri turned to Cyan and hissed something to her in their language. Whatever it was, her scales paled at his words. She looked back at Bron, eyes wide and slitted pupils barely visible. They continued their argument as the room spun more forcefully. Tobek drew Bron's left arm over his shoulder and gripped Bron's waist.

"Come on," Tobek said. "Let's all get back to the *Arrow*. It has a better medbay."

Tobek supported much of Bron's weight, helping him to stay upright. Olivia stuck close to his other side, only letting go of Bron's arm so that they could navigate the doorway more easily. As soon as they reached the wide hall, she hugged his right arm again.

"Is this because of…" she cast a quick glance at Tobek before turning back to Bron, "what was going on before? Or is it because of that stuff in the tank?"

"I don't know," Bron said, trying to clear his foggy thoughts.

The Vegans were right. Neither his biological nor his cybernetic parts should have let any of the tank's contents into his system. He thought back to the lockbox that had impacted his left leg when the *Reckoning* exploded and thrown his personal fighter into an uncontrolled spin. The errors within his systems had started after that. Bron had seen a scuff mark on the metal of his leg, but had thought little of it. His nanites should have repaired it. But what if they hadn't? What if it had provided an access point for whatever was in the tank?

"Perhaps both," he said.

Her lips thinned, and a wave of determination flowed from her, edging out her concern. She was coming up with a plan, and one that he might not like, based on her emotions. Before he could ask, they had passed through the airlock and were walking toward the ship. Bron's left leg buckled, the arm around Tobek's neck twitching hard enough to force the soldier to pause and hold on to Bron with both arms.

"We're almost there," Tobek said. "Cyan and Peri can help you."

The two Vegans exchanged a look that had Bron's hearts stuttering again. Uncertainty was clearly written across their features. Olivia caught it as well. She shook her head and stepped between them.

"We're not going to the *Arrow*," Olivia said.

"We will help him." Cyan stepped forward and took one of Olivia's hands in both of hers. "We will do everything we can."

"It won't be enough." Olivia shook her head. "You don't know what he was exposed to." She looked at Peri and said, "And you aren't familiar with his cybernetics."

"But—" Cyan began.

"She's right," Bron said. He appreciated Olivia trying

to keep his secret, though he was sure the Vegans must have their suspicions about the technology infused with his body. He still sensed that resolve within her, along with concern both for him and that he might not go along with whatever she had planned.

"We cannot leave the technology within this base unguarded," Peri said. "And we are not ready to bring in others to assess it. Not until we know more. The *Arrow* must remain here."

"Perhaps if they take a shard," Cyan said.

"We're not taking a shard." Olivia pulled away from Cyan and started waving both hands in the air. "Zemanni! I know you're still here."

"What?" Bron managed to stand straighter. "No. Absolutely not."

"It's the only way." She waved her arms again.

"He's a Scorpiian," Bron said. "They are not to be trusted."

"He's my friend," she turned on him defiantly, hands on hips. "And I do trust him."

Cyan stepped forward and said, "I also call Zemanni friend. And I trust him."

"This is insanity," Bron said.

"This is our only chance." Olivia grabbed his arm, her fingers cold against his burning skin. "If something happens to you, it happens to me. If whatever is going on with you kills you, I die, too. That's how it works, right?

We're bonded."

"You are bonded?" Cyan blinked big golden eyes at them. "When did you... Ugh, forget I asked."

Olivia smirked, then turned and waved one arm, keeping her grip on Bron with the other. "Come on, Zemanni," she shouted. "We need your help."

The space in front of them shimmered, revealing a large space ship hovering a few feet off the ground. A hatch opened beneath it and a ramp extended toward them. The ship maneuvered in a graceful arc, bringing the ramp closer. Energy crackled around them as the tunnel of atmosphere the *Arrow* was generating between it and the airlock to the base merged with another from Zemanni's ship.

Bron couldn't believe he was considering this. But Olivia's words were accurate. Whatever was wrong with him, it was serious and progressing quickly. The Vegans didn't know enough about his cybernetics, nor the many alterations that had been made to the rest of him to provide help. And if he died...

He looked into Olivia's dark, pleading eyes and felt another wave of determination from her. She would not take no for an answer. And he would not risk her life. Not even for his oath.

Chapter Thirteen

As soon as Tobek had helped Bron onto the ship, he left to join the others on the *Arrow*. Olivia stood next to her soulmate, stroking his hair as he leaned back in a chair in Zemanni's command center. Zemanni sat in front of them, his brow furrowed and his hands fused to the ship's controls.

The scar that wound around his neck glowed bright silver, as did the ones on his forearms. Olivia had heard rumors they were the result of a 'misunderstanding' he'd had with Craig and Barbara, a mated pair of enormous, four-armed Lyrians who had made Harbor their new home. She shuddered at the thought of what must have passed between them to leave such marks.

Zemanni's hands glowed with a soft silver light, his skin the same color and texture as liquid Mercury. The control panels he was using appeared to be made of a similar substance. She couldn't tell where the ship ended and Zemanni began. She had been so intent on getting to Bron, she hadn't paid much attention to Zemanni on the trip to Ceres. Now, seeing the lines of strain around the corners of his eyes, she wondered how much this journey was costing her friend.

The screen at the front of the room showed stone tunnels speeding past them as Zemanni navigated the ship out of the base on Ceres. Scorched metal was obvious in spots—evidence of the Cygnians' attack. Soon, dark rock gave way to millions of pinpricks of light. Olivia let out a breath when they cleared the asteroid belt and headed past Jupiter.

This was another thing she had missed on her journey to Ceres. She had been so distracted by thoughts of her soulmate, so focused on getting to him, that she hadn't let herself appreciate the wonder of traveling through her solar system. Now, as they passed Jupiter, she stared at the immense gaseous planet, watching the swirling patterns of color sweep across its surface. Her heart filled with awe.

"It's beautiful," she murmured.

"It's big," Zemanni said. "By that, I mean space is big. Want to narrow down our destination a bit?"

Bron gripped Olivia's hand and held it against his chest. His skin was burning up with fever and had taken on a strange greenish cast, moisture beading on his forehead. She wiped it away, leaning closer. Her heart ached for him. As far as she knew, Cygnians never fell ill. He'd already been through so much in his life. It didn't seem fair that he was dealing with this now.

"I can't tell him," Bron said.

"You have to." She bent down and kissed him. "Please.

I need you. And I'm not just talking about surviving. I need you, Bron."

"I know."

Olivia looked over at Zemanni. His hands detached from the controls as he rose. Rather than join them, he stayed where he was, leaning against the back of his chair with his arms crossed. He stared at Bron intently, his dark brows furrowed. The scar surrounding Zemanni's neck pulsed with silver light and lines of strain stood out around his eyes that she'd never seen before.

"We can do a void run," he said.

"A what?" Olivia asked.

"A void run," he repeated. "I've done them before. You put the coordinates on an encrypted slip that I then enter into my ship's navigation system, bypassing the computer entirely. Gets us there and back with no record of where we went."

"That sounds perfect." She smiled at Bron, but he shook his head. "Oh, come on. We have to get there. Bron…"

"Don't blame him," Zemanni said. "Between the Cygnian's overdeveloped sense of 'honor' and the secretive nature of the Psiarae, he'd probably rather let himself die if you weren't part of the equation."

"How do you know…" Bron said, his usually deep voice thready.

"Please." Zemanni snorted. "If you turned to me, that

means the Vegans can't help you. And a Cygnian cyborg? You have Psiarae stamped all over you."

"He already knows," Olivia pleaded. "Let him take us there. You don't even have to tell him where to go."

Bron let out a sigh, then closed his eyes. At first, Olivia thought he was refusing, or maybe that he'd lost consciousness. His breathing quickened, his brows drawing together, then a low hum vibrated through the ship. She looked over at Zemanni to see him standing straight, glancing all around with his mouth open in surprise. He snapped it shut when their eyes met, then sat in his chair and placed his hands on his command panels. His hands glowed bright silver, but the panels remained solid beneath him.

"What the hell are you doing with my ship?" Zemanni demanded.

"Starting the void run," Bron said.

The screen at the front of the room flickered, the stars going dark. Then an inky blue spread across it, like water dropped in oil. The lights dimmed and a high whine rang through the air, loud enough to make her ears ache. Her heartbeat picked up as the floor beneath her vibrated ominously.

"Bron…" Zemanni said, in a warning voice.

Bron's eyebrows were pinched together. More sweat coursed down his temples into his hair. Olivia ran her hand over his forehead, his skin almost burning her. Finally, his features relaxed, and he sank deeper into the chair, letting out a long breath. The blue on the screen brightened, swirling around them in rich cobalt and deep sapphire tones that sped past them. Olivia had heard people talk about blue space, but had never dreamt she'd be on a ship traveling through it.

Zemanni swiveled his chair around to stare at them. "That's a neat trick."

Bron shrugged. "I don't have a slip on me to input the coordinates."

"That wasn't the smoothest entry into blue space I've ever had," Zemanni said.

"Your ship wasn't forthcoming." Bron closed his eyes.

"What's that supposed to mean?" Zemanni said.

"The specs are off." The furrow between Bron's brows deepened again. "We hit some turbulence because the shape and weight didn't match your ship's design data."

Zemanni just grunted.

"What a shock," Bron said. "A Scorpiian keeping secrets."

"Yeah, like you're an open book." Zemanni leaned back in his chair. "I've been studying you Cygnians since you started moving onto my planet."

"*Your* planet?" Olivia arched an eyebrow. She knew Scorpiians were territorial with each other, but not that their mindsets included the other aliens colonizing Earth.

"Nobody has any idea you're a cyborg." Zemanni

continued as if she hadn't spoken. "Not even your prism. Hell, the Vegans couldn't even tell. You, my friend, are *made* of secrets."

"I'm not your friend," Bron snapped, lifting his head so he could glare at Zemanni.

"Hey." Olivia stood straighter next to Bron. She knew he didn't like Scorpiians, like so many aliens she'd met, but that didn't mean he could be rude. Especially when Zemanni was doing them such a huge favor. "Zemanni is my friend, and he's helping us. I get that you're hurting, but don't take it out on him."

Bron took in a deep breath, then let it out slowly. "You're right. I apologize."

"Well, that's a new one," Zemanni said, eyeing Bron with a bemused expression. He looked around the command room, then asked, "How long is this little trip going to take?"

"Get comfortable," Bron said.

"Great," Zemanni murmured. "Are you going to keep me locked out of my controls the whole time?"

"I programmed a failsafe." Bron closed his eyes and let out a long breath. "The ship will return to Earth in one week and then give over full control to you. I suggest you be on it then."

"A week?" Zemanni shook his head. "Brooke is going to be pissed."

"Brooke?" Bron said.

Olivia leaned close and whispered, "His girlfriend."

Bron's eyebrows rose and Olivia laughed, hoping to ease some of the tension in the room. Zemanni's scowl deepened.

"Don't look so surprised," Zemanni said. "Earthlings are appealing, as I'm sure you understand."

"I certainly do." Bron lifted Olivia's hand, threading their fingers together and bringing it to his lips for a kiss.

Zemanni rose from his chair and approached them. Bron's grip tightened and his expression turned wary.

"Oh, give it a rest, already," Olivia said.

"Yes, Bron, give it a rest." Zemanni smirked when he reached the wall next to Bron's chair. "Or at least give Olivia a place to rest." He lifted his hand to one of the smooth command panels on the wall and said, "May I?"

Bron's eyes narrowed, but then he glanced over at Olivia. She nodded, focusing on her trust for Zemanni and the warm feelings of friendship she had for him. Bron scowled, but then relaxed and turned away. The command panel rippled, fusing with Zemanni's hand.

"Thank you," Zemanni said. He turned to the wall and concentrated, the lines around his eyes deepening.

Was it always this hard for him to control his own ship? It didn't seem like it should take him this much effort. Olivia watched over him as well, ready to assist if he needed it. At least, she intended to. A column of molten silver rose from the floor, drawing her attention. It ballooned out, lengthening and flattening until it formed another chair right next to Bron's. The chair was angled so that she could watch him while she sat in it.

"Thank you," Olivia said.

Zemanni detached himself from the control panel and shrugged. "Since we're going to be awhile." He stared at Bron, smirking as he returned to his own chair, then sat and leaned back, eyes shut.

Olivia climbed into the chair, pleased with how close she could stay to her soulmate. Bron was glaring at Zemanni.

"I don't like him," Bron said.

Olivia laughed. "He gets that a lot. But he grows on you."

Bron let out a disgruntled snort. She reached out and smoothed his hair away from his face. His skin wasn't as hot as before and the odd greenish cast was gone. His normal blue was washed out, but he looked... better.

"How are you feeling?" she asked.

"I'm fine."

She sighed. "Seriously. I need to know."

"I should have thought to make you a chair," Bron said.

She smiled and laughed again, pleased that he could focus on something so trivial. Surely, that was a sign that he wasn't still suffering.

"You were probably thinking I could just crawl up in there with you," she said, gesturing toward his chair.

"Now that you mention it…"

Olivia leaned in for a kiss, but Zemanni let out a groan. Bron growled as she pulled back, smiling.

She arched a brow and said, "Any chance you can make this thing go any faster?"

In that sexy low voice of his, Bron said, "I'll do my best."

Chapter Fourteen

By the time they reached the Psiarae homeworld, Bron felt almost himself again. At least, in biological terms. That static was still hovering in the background of both his senses and sensors. But his body seemed to have purged itself of whatever contaminants Norem's serum had introduced. Bron was glad he could walk into the Psiarae's city on his own two feet.

He kept the screen dark as he dropped Zemanni's ship out of blue space. It was much less turbulent now that he knew the computer held inaccurate data. Bron supposed it made sense for a mercenary and smuggler to alter his ship's records, in case he was waylaid and inspected by authorities. Which authorities could capture a Scorpiian vessel, Bron had no idea.

As much as he wished to share the beauty of this part of space with Olivia, Bron couldn't let the others see anything about the Psiarae home system that might give them clues that would lead them back to this sector. He stood in the middle of the command room, feet braced in a warrior's stance, arms folded over his bare chest, and eyes closed so that he could focus on their approach to the planet.

Merging his consciousness with the ship felt oddly natural. It was as though he was the one flying through the system, weaving past green-hued gas giants. He had experienced nothing like it before, unwilling to risk detection by his prism. Expanding his awareness beyond himself, feeling the ship as if it was his own body... It was nearly euphoric. Especially when he felt the supple metal of his own cybernetics beneath the biological arm locked across his chest.

He had never once stood like this without his tunic. Had never felt what of him was Cygnian and what was cyborg together, integrated. He hadn't felt whole physically since his childhood accident. Not until this moment. And now, he was spiritually whole as well.

Olivia stood at his side, her warmth and love feeding into him, a constant stream of support and acceptance. She hadn't left his side for more than a few moments in the near day that it had taken to reach the Psiarae system— what the Earthlings called the constellation Pisces. With her strength adding to his own, they could accomplish anything. He was sure of it.

Gamma Piscium 1, the Psiarae homeworld, loomed in front of them. A shell of bright aqua glaciers encased the planet. Beneath the layer of ice was water that plunged to depths as dark as the farthest reaches of space.

Bron hadn't been able to get a new pair of wristbands

from the *Arrow*. Earth's oceans were intimidating enough, knowing that the density of Cygnian bodies made them sink. At least with their wristbands, they could walk along the bottom of whatever water they found themselves in and eventually reach land—if the charge on their wristbands held. Cygnian technology fed on light, and there was none in the depths of the Psiarae's oceanic homeworld.

He and his prism were always careful to approach planets from above large land masses, such as the ones that graced Earth's surface. Gamma Piscium 1's icy terrain would be survivable with wristbands, but knowing what lurked beneath and how thin certain areas of the ice could be… Bron's spine plates rose at the thought of it.

He couldn't let fear keep him from what he knew he needed to do. The Psiarae didn't live on the surface. They lived deep below. His nanites were equipped with something of a homing beacon that Bron was following to their place of origin.

"Your ship can handle underwater travel, correct?" Bron said, without opening his eyes.

"To a point." Zemanni's voice was close. Olivia had been right. Bron was already getting used to his proximity.

"Are the specs accurate about the amount of pressure it can handle?" Bron asked.

He hated having to share even that much about the Psiarae homeworld, but at least Zemanni only knew now that underwater travel was involved. He knew nothing of the starkly beautiful surface that stretched beneath him, mountains of ice rising that Bron deftly navigated the ship between. They were very similar to the crystal mountains of his homeworld, the icy sphere on their planet's surface mimicking the crystal shell that protected Cygnus-Prime from its neighboring black hole. Perhaps it wasn't such a stretch to see why his own queen Ehmach had some sort of relationship with the leader of the Psiarae. Their worlds held interesting parallels.

"If the specs are off, they're lower than maximum capacity," Zemanni said.

"That's what I thought."

Bron took a deep breath, dropping his arms to his sides. One with the ship, he flew up in a huge, circling arc. At the zenith of the curve, he raised his shields and engaged his engines fully. A rush of power flowed through him as the ship's systems complied. The icy surface sped toward him. His hearts pounded faster, bringing Olivia's along with their eager beat. Just before the nose of the vessel hit the ice, Bron fired all the forward lasers. The ship plunged through the weakened area, cracking through its solid icy surface. The water began to re-freeze immediately, sealing them below.

A shiver passed through him, his spine plates vibrating in strong pulses. Water pressed on him, currents pulling at the ship. Panic edged in around the edges of his thought.

Warmth pushed it back. Olivia was at his side, her fingers lacing with his. He drew on her strength, pulled his consciousness back from the ship until he stood in the command center once more. The water still lurked just beyond the ship's walls. He did his best to ignore it, telling the ship where to go to reach the Psiarae city. Finally, he opened his eyes to see the room around him.

Zemanni was staring with open curiosity. His arms were crossed, as well as his ankles, as he leaned against the far wall of the room. Olivia was hugging Bron's right arm. She stared up at him with wide, worried eyes.

"You were so far away from me," she said.

"Never." He dusted his finger across her cheekbone. "I am always with you."

She shook her head. "There was... something else."

"The ship," he said. "I merged my consciousness with its systems."

"I didn't like it." She stopped him when he was about to speak. "I know it was necessary, but... It felt as if there was a wall between us. It was the same as before we bonded."

"Next time it is necessary, I will be certain to let you know in advance and to reassure you." He wrapped an arm around her waist and pulled her close, smiling as he projected his desire for her.

She smiled back, one hand against his chest. "I look forward to that."

"Get a room," Zemanni said.

"What?" Bron asked.

"He means we need some privacy," Olivia whispered.

"Ah." Bron nodded, then turned to Zemanni and said, "Leave."

Zemanni let out a disgusted snort. "It's *my* ship. And you are not doing *that* on my bridge."

"Fine." Bron hadn't been serious, but it was interesting to see the Scorpiian lose a bit of his composure.

"Want to give us a look at where we are?" Zemanni asked.

Bron chuckled. "Certainly."

He activated the screen, revealing the pitch black of the surrounding water. Zemanni looked at the screen, then back to Bron, scowling.

"Charming," Zemanni said.

"Wait, what's that?" Olivia stepped closer to the display, squinting at a speck of blue. It grew larger as they approached. "Oh my god."

Bron hadn't been to Psiaraht, the principal city of the Psiarae, since he was a child. He had never seen it from outside and only had vague, fractured memories of smooth, white walls within and aqua lights running along the ceilings with bubbles that travelled through them.

Ehmach had argued constantly with the Psiaraen leader, Tethis. Whenever Bron had been conscious, it seemed the women were at each other's throats. He had always wondered what the Cygnians could have done that would make the Psiarae so in their debt that they would give some of their technology to Bron. Seeing the city emerge from the inky depths gave him his answer.

The city was made entirely of crystal. Beautiful, meticulously cultivated Cygnian crystal that sprang from the bottom of the ocean and grew in enormous and complex clusters, forming buildings connected by tunnels made of the same aqua-hued stone. Lights from within the structures illuminated their crystal walls, making the city appear as a spectacular beacon in the darkness. The Psiarae might call this home, but the city was unmistakably Cygnian in design.

"It's breathtaking," Olivia said.

"It's Cygnian." Zemanni cast a knowing look at Bron.

Olivia turned to him. "Really?"

"It is," Bron said.

She looked back at the screen. "It looks like your people and the Psiarae might be closer than you thought."

Bron had his doubts. He kept them to himself as he piloted the ship beneath one of the pressurized bays, slowly edging up until the top of the ship breached the water and was exposed to a section of the city that held air. The ship's sensors told him it was breathable for all three of them. That didn't mean the Psiarae couldn't flood the space with toxic gases—or just water—if they weren't in a welcoming mood. They were an aquatic species well suited for their oceanic homeworld. Zemanni might be able to change form to breathe underwater, and Olivia's wristbands would keep her safe for a time, but Bron... His spine plates vibrated more intensely at the thought of all that water surrounding them.

Aside from breathing, there was also the matter of the incredible pressure at these depths. Again, reaching out through the ship's sensors, he could tell that the bay wasn't just pressurized to keep the water out. They must have dropped the levels significantly for their 'guests.' The Psiarae themselves could handle extreme pressure and cold. It was, again, an encouraging thought that they had made this space so accommodating to others. Perhaps their isolationist culture had mellowed.

A large door opened at the end of the hangar bay and dozens of Psiarae marched within, moving in orderly rows. Each was wearing an encounter suit, the light gleaming off the oily dark metal and seeming to be pulled in by the navy blue of the flexible fabric between the joints of their body armor.

Bron was certain each suit was outfitted with all the abilities they had infused into his body with his cybernetics—and even more. Weapons systems, antigravity boosters... He could think of countless ways those suits would make the Psiarae even more deadly. Something about the design was reminiscent of the Vegans' exosuits. His hearts sped up, but he willed them back under control. It was never wise to show fear.

The soldiers' faces were visible within glass domes, their features somewhat distorted by the liquid within. Bron was surprised at how similar their appearance was to his own species, as well as Sadirians and Earthlings. Aside from their pale aqua skin and large, almost glowing, bright blue eyes, they could be mistaken for any of those sentients. Without their helmets, the gills beneath their jaws and the frills on their pointed ears would set them apart, as well as their claw-tipped, webbed fingers and toes.

Another party of Psiarae entered the room. Four were elite guards, their body armor a bright aqua, but still having that unsettling movement within the color. The two women walking in front held Bron's attention. Tall and thin, these Psiarae didn't wear encounter suits. Instead, tight, rubbery fabric encased their bodies. The material was so white, it almost seemed to give off its own light. They wore collars of the same bright aqua material as their guards' encounter suits. The devices let out puffs of mist periodically near their gills.

Without helmets, the women's features were even more similar to other familiar sentients. Perhaps they were a bit more delicate and muted. Their lips were thin and wide, bright turquoise hair flowed behind them as if moving through water. They resembled each other enough that Bron was certain they were mother and daughter. The older woman, who he believed to be their leader, Tethis, wore a long white cloak that brushed her ankles. She clasped her hands in front of her and regarded the ship with a severe frown.

"Exit your vessel." Her voice was high and commanding, the sound reverberating within the crystal confines of the hangar bay. A sense of tension flowed along with it, the soldiers drawing themselves up into stances of readiness.

"What do we do?" Olivia asked.

"Obey," Bron said.

Chapter Fifteen

"I'm staying with my ship." Zemanni glared at Bron defiantly.

The last thing they needed was for Zemanni and Bron to start arguing. Olivia's heart was pounding, though its beat was steady. She could sense Bron willing himself to remain calm, but an unsettling amount of anxiety lurked beneath the veneer he projected.

"They'll be able to sense you within," Bron said. "The Psiarae are quick to take offense and will think nothing of destroying your ship with you in it. They're probably just looking for an excuse."

"And tell me again why we came here?" Zemanni leaned forward, his scowl deepening.

"Because you're my friend." Olivia's stomach clenched as she realized what a dangerous situation she had dragged Zemanni into. She hadn't known coming to this planet would be such a risk. "And because Bron needs their help."

Zemanni shook his head, then pushed himself away from the wall where he'd been leaning. "Fine. Let's go."

Olivia took Bron's hand and together they followed

Zemanni through a short series of passageways to the back of the ship. Each step filled her with more apprehension. Why were the Psiarae putting on such a show of force? If the Cygnians had built this city for them and helped save Bron, why did they appear so hostile now? Her mind was spinning when Zemanni stopped next to a large hatch.

"Do you want to do the honors?" he said, gesturing toward the control panel.

Bron took a deep breath, then let it out. The hatch slid open, and a ramp began extending from the ship toward the floor of the hangar bay they were in. His hand tightened around hers.

The view before her was incredible. The aqua crystal extended within the interior structure of the city as well, forming a high dome above them. Light gleamed off of the smooth white floors, reflecting from some sort of light fixtures hanging on the walls. The entire space was immense. Water lapped at the sides of Zemanni's ship, dark and putting off a chill that should have made her shiver. She wondered if the wristbands Bron had given her were insulating her from the temperature while somehow letting her experience it, the way they had protected her while letting her feel him when they bonded. Her skin prickled from the odd sensation of feeling the cold, yet not suffering from it.

"Whatever happens, do not shut down the shielding or atmospheric generators of your wristbands," Bron said.

"That's not as reassuring as you might think," she muttered. "Won't these things eventually run out of power?"

"The ambient light is sufficient to maintain their charge," Bron said. "And I hope not to be here long."

"You and me both." Zemanni headed down the ramp first. He stood to one side so that Olivia and Bron could join him before the Psiarae.

Even with all her practice dealing with aliens in Harbor, it was difficult not to stare. The women before her were gorgeous in an ethereal manner. They were taller than Olivia and Zemanni, but not as tall as Bron. Their limbs were long and graceful, as were their torsos. The way they held themselves reminded her of ballerinas. The older woman had the slightest creases at the edges of her eyes, while the younger stared at Olivia with open curiosity. Olivia smiled at her, and the girl smiled back.

If Olivia hadn't already figured they were mother and daughter, she would have been sure of it when the older woman made an odd trilling sound and somehow cast a glare at her daughter without turning to face her. The younger Psiarae bowed her head and took a step back, folding her hands in front of her. At least they knew not all the Psiarae were upset by their presence.

"Bron," the older woman said.

"Tethis." Bron lifted both hands to his chest, holding them as fists above each heart, then bowed slightly.

"Why are you here?" she demanded.

"I have sustained damage," Bron said. "My nanites are unable to make repairs."

"Preposterous." She let out another odd trill, this one even more full of contempt than the first. "You appear functional. I ask you again, why are you here?"

"Please, he *is* hurt," Olivia said, stepping forward.

Tethis stiffened, recoiling without stepping back. Olivia lowered her head in what she hoped would be seen as deference or respect. Bron placed his right arm over her shoulder. A wave of warmth and love flowed through her, along with a surge of pride. Though he didn't look at her, she could sense his encouragement and stood straighter.

"The effects are intermittent," Bron said. "I would not have come if the situation was not dire."

Tethis narrowed her eyes. "You come here at your own peril."

"'Our own peril?'" Olivia said. "So, you go from having the Cygnians build this incredible city for you—making you a *home*—to them being in danger if they come to visit?"

"The scales are balanced between us," Tethis said. "Ehmach called in the favor that was owed between our people in asking us to rebuild this one." She angled her head at Bron, condescension thick in her tone. "We were not to be approached again."

"Your people are linked," Olivia said. "Don't you see

that? The Cygnians created this place. What if you need repairs? Or to expand?"

Tethis made her disapproving trill again, then said, "Who are you?"

"This is Olivia," Bron said. "My soulmate."

"Soulmate?" The younger woman stepped forward, her eyes wide with wonder. Before she could approach closer, her mother flung her arm up between them.

"Iridia," she snapped.

The girl jumped, then bowed her head and stepped back, her expression shuttering. Olivia bit the inside of her cheek to keep from yelling at Tethis. Just because she was Iridia's mother didn't mean she could bully her. But Olivia didn't want to make the situation worse. She cast a sympathetic look at Iridia, who returned it with a slight smile.

"You should not have come," Tethis said. "You know of our ways."

"I had no choice," Bron said.

"And did you also have no choice in telling these outsiders of our role in this?" she demanded. "In bringing *them* here?"

"I'm his soulmate." Olivia's temper was getting the best of her. "I wasn't about to let him face this alone. And this is Zemanni's ship." Olivia said, gesturing behind them. "We needed it to get here."

"Zemanni…" Tethis angled her head. Her skin began to

strobe with bright white and aqua lights as she stepped in front of Iridia, using her cloak to fully block her daughter from view. Every soldier behind her shifted into a fighting stance, their movements uncannily linked.

"Relax," Zemanni said. "I'm retired."

"How dare you bring a Scorpiian here!" Tethis yelled.

"Technically, they didn't bring me here." Zemanni shrugged. "*My ship*. I brought them."

Olivia swayed on her feet, the room spinning around her. She tried to... do something. What was she doing? Where was she? Olivia couldn't look away from the woman putting off the beautiful lights. Bron tightened his grip on her, a deep rumble vibrating out from his chest. The room dimmed around her. At first, she thought it was her vision, but then she realized she could see the shielding from her wristbands. The gold light brightened, muting the strobing lights Tethis was putting off.

"Tethis, stop." Bron's low voice was thick with warning. His spine plates stood on end, their vibration somehow helping Olivia to feel more herself. "We may not be allies in your mind, but I know you do not want the Cygnians as your enemies."

The Psiarae's skin returned to normal, her shoulders lowering. Behind her, the soldiers' stances became less overtly aggressive.

"What just happened?" Olivia shook her head to clear it further.

"My reputation preceded me," Zemanni said, his trademark smirk in full force. "That's what."

"What reputation?" Olivia knew other aliens treated Zemanni differently—even the Vegans, except for Cyan. They all avoided him and changed the subject if he came up in conversation. She only knew him as a somewhat smug, coffee-addicted guy who loved books as much as video games.

The only other Scorpiian she knew anything about was Dean. He was a mercenary who had been causing trouble on Earth, including ordering someone to abduct a Lyrian infant. Lian was babysitting the nestling at the time and had been taken, too. Fortunately, Nuar and the other Cygnians had rescued them both. If the town's rumor-mill was to be believed, Dean had also been behind the recent destruction of the *Reckoning*. There had even been Public Service Announcement videos made about him, warning the citizens of Harbor and giving them tips on how to protect themselves. It had all seemed somewhat ridiculous. Seeing how seriously these people were taking Zemanni as a threat, Olivia was starting to rethink that.

"Zemanni is a good man," Olivia said.

"He is an assassin," Tethis said. "And you are a fool."

"I'm not here on a mission." Zemanni took a step to one side and every soldier in the room shifted to keep him in their line of sight.

Crap, they *were* taking him seriously. Was he really an

assassin? Dean was just a mercenary, and the Department of Homeworld Security back on Earth was treating him as though he was a major threat. How was it they were fine working with Zemanni?

Zemanni's smirk deepened, as if their unease pleased him. Olivia gave him a stern look, and some of the smugness left his expression. Only some.

"I'm just helping a friend," Zemanni said.

"You have nothing to fear from him," Bron said. "He can't shapeshift anymore."

Every trace of smugness left Zemanni's face. His mouth pulled into a grimacing frown and the lines at the corners of his eyes deepened as if he was in pain. The line of silver around his neck pulsed brighter. More lines of light glowed faintly beneath his clothing, on his legs, arms, and even his torso. How many of those scars did he have?

"Preposterous," Tethis said.

"An enraged Lyrian ripped him to pieces," Bron said. "It's incredible that he was able to put himself back together and survive this long."

My god...

Was that true? She wanted to reach out to her friend, to comfort him. However, now was not the time.

"You're missing the bigger issue here," Zemanni said, his voice strained. "Bron's cybernetics have been compromised. *Your technology* has been compromised. Aren't you even the slightest bit concerned about how that happened?"

Tethis narrowed her eyes, a deep trill emanating from her. She turned back to Bron, looking him up and down as if studying him for the first time.

"What injured you?" she asked.

"A shockwave hit my personal fighter while I was transporting something," Bron said. "The turbulence caused it to impact my left leg. Somehow, it penetrated the metal. My nanites sought to repair the damage at first, but sent error messages and they refuse to approach that area now. My cybernetics have been glitching ever since. It's like a virus was introduced to my systems that I can't purge."

"And then you were also exposed to Norem's serum, which affected your biological systems," Olivia said. She could sense that he wasn't pleased with her sharing that information, but she knew patients would sometimes leave out vital information. "They need to know everything if they're going to help you."

"You certainly come to us presenting several problems," Tethis said. "What of this item you were transporting that introduced the mechanical virus? What are its origins?"

Bron looked at Zemanni uneasily, then said, "It was a Scorpiian lockbox."

Chapter Sixteen

"And how convenient that a Scorpiian has brought you to us," Tethis said.

Bron had hoped to avoid sharing that bit of information for just this reason. The Psiarae had become even more isolationist since they had helped him, it seemed. Almost paranoid. Then again, even he saw the entire situation as suspicious. If it weren't for Olivia's faith in Zemanni, Bron would question his involvement.

"It's actually pretty damned inconvenient." Zemanni glared at Bron. "Seeing that he didn't bother to share that information with me."

"It didn't seem relevant," Bron said

Zemanni snorted. "All of our lockboxes are trapped. If someone touches it whose DNA doesn't match the owner's, the trap is triggered."

"Many of us handled it without issue," Bron said.

"Yeah, because our technology can't pierce your thick Cygnian hides." Zemanni shook his head. "But I'd wager the metal of that leg isn't as invulnerable."

"What does the trap do when it's triggered?" Olivia asked, her concern mounting.

"Most have a long-lasting paralytic poison in them," Zemanni said. "The box alerts the owner that someone is messing with it and sends a location beacon so the owner can show up and deal with whoever it is."

"A biological poison would not affect cybernetic systems." Tethis angled her head again, a bit of curiosity creeping into her expression. "You present an interesting puzzle to us." She straightened and said, "Very well. We will examine you and enact repairs if we are able. Your companions shall remain here, where our soldiers can monitor them."

"But…" Olivia stepped forward, but Bron caught her shoulders and held her in place.

"It's safer here," he said. "You'll be close to the ship."

Though Tethis was apparently intrigued by the problem he presented, he wasn't sure if she would let him leave again—or let any of them leave. She could study him, then decide it was too much of a risk to let them go. Bron doubted she would kill him. The other members of his prism would sense that, and they would go to the queen. He was certain Ehmach would figure out where he had gone, and then there would be war between the Cygnians and the Psiarae.

It was more likely that Tethis would keep him here. If she tried to do so, Bron wanted Olivia to get to the safety of the ship quickly. Even if he was trapped here, she could escape. As long as he survived, so would she. The thought of being separated tore at his hearts, but her survival was more important than anything.

Bron leaned down and pressed his lips to hers. She wrapped her arms around his neck as he deepened the kiss. All too soon, he had to pull away.

"I will always find my way back to you," he said. "Remember that."

She nodded, her eyes glassy. "You just get better."

He nodded, unable to release her hands as he stepped back. Bron glared at Zemanni and said, "Keep her safe."

"Sure," the Scorpiian said.

Bron wished they had more time, but Tethis turned and said, "Follow me."

He gently squeezed Olivia's hands once more, then followed the Psiarae and her cluster of guards. Her daughter cast a furtive smile at Olivia as they headed out of the hangar area through the archway where the soldiers had entered. Glancing over his shoulder, Bron saw they had all remained behind, guarding the ship and watching Zemanni, no doubt. The thought rankled Bron oddly. Was he starting to trust the Scorpiian? Or was he feeling an echo of Olivia's feelings for her friend?

Iridia was staring at him when he turned his attention back to the pair before him. Her smile brightened when they made eye contact, and he couldn't keep himself from returning it, despite his grim circumstances. Here was a Psiarae who didn't seem as xenophobic as their leader. Her mother made a sharp trill, and Iridia started, her smile faltering. She nodded, then bowed her head and darted down a hallway that branched off from the side of the main corridor. Apparently, she had been dismissed.

He should have contacted Ehmach before coming here. But there had been no time. At least, it had seemed that way. His strength had returned to him, though, and the horrible sensations flooding his body had lessened. Even the loss of motor control in his cybernetic limbs had subsided for the moment. Could Norem's serum have affected even them? Norem had been working on creating cyborgs. Perhaps the fluid contained nanites as well as whatever genetic cocktail the mad Tau Ceti had conjured up. Bron's spine plates tried to rise at the thought, but he kept them clamped to his back, his muscles straining from the effort. He didn't want the Psiarae to know the depth of his unease.

They led him through white-walled corridors, gracefully curving above them to form the ceiling. A line of aqua light ran along the highest point of the arcing ceiling, parallel to their path. The same bubbles he remembered from his youth traveled within the tubes of glowing liquid. Had they drained the corridor of water for him, or was this entire section of the city always pressurized for air-breathing lifeforms?

Bron looked at the floors and along the walls and didn't see any openings where water could be removed—or added, reassuringly. It seemed strange for a reclusive species to have such a large area be inhospitable to themselves. But then, Cygnians had created the city. Perhaps they had built this section for their own use while completing their work.

Tethis paused before a doorway, then waved her hand over a control panel. The door slid open. Bron's spine plates snapped up, their vibration sending a pulse through the air surrounding him. He couldn't stop them this time. All his strength was going toward not backing away from the room within.

He remembered this place.

Several laboratory beds stretched out from the walls, spinning lights hovering above them as they waited for patients. Once someone lay down on the beds—or was placed there—the holographic projectors would spring to life and provide continuous diagnostic scans of the patient's body. Bron had been on one of these beds. He had seen the holograms of his body, of the damage that had been done and of what had been missing. Almost half of his body. Gone.

His hearts pounded and his mouth went dry as memories flooded his mind.

'Don't open your eyes,' he thought. 'I don't want to see.'

But his eyes fluttered open, seemingly of their own

volition. Above him, the aqua light of the hologram was almost familiar. It was the same as the displays his teachers used in school. The same he had studied before going on the hunt for the beryl beast. The beast who had...

Bron clenched his eyes shut, tears streaming from them. He heard movement nearby. The odd burbling of the engineers' encounter suits. The soft hum of machinery.

'I'm going to be a machine.'

"You are a Cygnian warrior," someone said, her voice close at his side.

Yes. He was. He would still be, even after this.

"Warriors do not flinch from battle." Her hand clasped his, tethering him to his body. What was left of it.

He opened his eyes, staring at the image above him. Panic rose, his heart pounding. Only one. Why could he only feel one?

"Control the fear. Push it away from you."

All he felt was fear. If he pushed it away, what would he have left? What did he have left already? He closed his eyes, unable to look at the scans anymore.

"Control the fear." Someone squeezed his right hand. "Push it away."

How much time passed before he opened his eyes again? His body had changed. A second leg rested in the space on the bed that had been empty before. Not attached. Not yet. Someone bent over him, doing things to his hip that sent odd chills through his body. He couldn't lift his head to see them fully, more sensing them than anything. But he could see what they were doing on the scan.

Devices snaked through his torso and across his pelvis, bright white lines of cabling with instruments attached to their ends. Flashes of energy illuminated the spots where they worked, each burst of light corresponding to another of those unsettling chills. The leg shifted closer. Not his leg. A mechanical one. Artificial.

'I don't want to be a machine.'

Alerts sounded. Red lights flared angrily within his torso on the scan above.

The voice at his side spoke again, somehow both urgent and calm. Her hand still clutched his. "You are a Cygnian warrior. Fight for your life. Fight."

He closed his eyes and took a deep breath, pushing the panic away. 'I am a Cygnian warrior.'

When he opened his eyes again, the leg was attached to his hip. From the waist down, he almost looked whole. Except that his left leg and part of that hip gleamed white, his biological parts a pale blue.

'There is so much white...'

Movement caught his attention. He could see the people working on him now. A male and a female, their rich turquoise hair covered with stark white fabric that kept it from their faces. Their eyes were enormous, their lips and noses thin. Dark metal collars wrapped around each of their necks, letting out occasional puffs of mist. Each time, gills appeared beneath their jaws, sucking in the vapor. They spoke in hushed whispers.

The man glanced up at him and caught Bron's eyes. He smiled. Reaching up, he brushed his webbed fingers over Bron's forehead.

The voice spoke at his side again, his other side. "This is the greatest battle you will ever face."

'I am a Cygnian warrior.'

This time, he didn't need to hear the woman's voice prompting him. Bron pushed aside his fear, his dread, his... everything. A cold calm settled over his thoughts. He looked back at the scans, studying them as if he was watching the procedures being performed on someone else. Detaching himself from all the emotions surrounding what had happened. What continued to happen.

They had encased his left heart in some sort of flexible material that flowed down the torn remnants of the left side of his torso to keep the organs in place. Bron watched as the man and woman rebuilt his ribs, his chest, his abdomen. Gleaming metal spread across his chest. More of the flexible material stretched between the metal panels, presumably to grant him a full range of motion. Each stage of his repair was accompanied by an infusion of nanites and each infusion spread more chills through him.

'This is the greatest battle I will ever face. I am still a Cygnian warrior. I am still me.'

Finally, they finished attaching his left arm. The hologram above showed his body complete, gleaming blue and stark white light showing what was biological and what was machine. The man and woman looked at someone standing on his right side, their voices low and full of warning.

"The nanites need to integrate with his brain to give him full control of his new anatomy," the man said. "This includes building a central processing unit. It will take time and... We cannot deaden the pain."

"He may also reject the systems we have installed." The woman's voice was colder, with an edge of annoyance to it. "In which case, he will die."

The man turned to her and made a series of angry trilling sounds. The woman frowned at him in response.

"You will not die," the voice at his side said. "You have come too far for that."

The man looked at whoever was standing at Bron's side, his mouth pulled in a grim line. "This next part... It will not be pleasant." He turned back to Bron, his aqua eyes narrowed with purpose. "Do you understand?"

Bron felt moisture escape the edges of his eyes, but he felt no fear. The surrounding air vibrated, the feeling familiar, resonating through the right side of his body. His hand was held in a tight grasp still. He looked over to see Ehmach beside him, her spine plates standing straight up from her back. The fierce orange glow of her eyes was blurred by the tears in his own.

"I am a Cygnian warrior," Bron said. "I'm ready."

Chapter Seventeen

Olivia was going crazy. She hugged herself tight as she paced in front of the several dozen soldiers in the hangar. They didn't even bother her anymore. No, she was too distracted even to care about their presence. Bron needed her. Wherever he was, she could sense his need, his fear.

This place... The worst memories of his life had happened here. She could imagine too well what he had gone through. The accident had probably felt surreal. The initial trauma and shock would have insulated him from what was happening, but here... He would have had time to think, time to process, and time to understand what had happened, what he had lost. It was the same as when she walked into the hospital where they had taken her after her own accident.

Olivia should have gone with him. Should have insisted on it. Bron needed her, and she couldn't get to him.

"To hell with this," she said.

She started toward the door. Half a dozen soldiers moved to intercept her, standing between her and the exit. Between her and Bron.

"Get out of my way," she said.

Zemanni caught her arm and pulled her back. "Don't antagonize them. Bron knows what he's doing. He'll be back soon."

"You don't know that," she said. "You don't know anything."

His frown deepened.

"I'm sorry." She shook her head. "You didn't deserve that. But I can feel him out there. I know he needs me. I have to get to him. It's like... I don't know how to describe it. It's something I can't control."

"Return to your ranks." Iridia swept into the room, waving an arm toward the soldiers. They hesitated, then went back to their places, facing the ship.

"You will come with me." Her voice was imperious, much more like her mother's.

"Where are you taking us?" Olivia asked.

Iridia glanced at the soldiers, then stepped closer. She lowered her voice a bit and said, "To your soulmate."

Olivia's heart pounded. She wasn't sure if it was from her own emotions or whatever Bron was dealing with. All she knew was that she would do anything to get to him.

"Lead the way," she said.

"Olivia," Zemanni said.

"You don't have to come," Olivia said. "But I'm going."

Zemanni sighed, then gestured toward the door. "After

you." He fell in step beside Olivia as they hurried from the hangar.

"I can't take you to him directly," Iridia said. "My mother wouldn't approve of you being with him."

"Neither would Bron," Zemanni said.

Olivia ignored him. "Why are you doing this, then?"

"Because you're soulmates," Iridia said. "You belong together."

It was true. Olivia belonged at Bron's side. She should never have let him go off to face this without her.

Iridia led them through a maze of corridors, finally stopping in front of a small door. She waved her hand over a control panel next to it and the door slid open.

"Quickly, before a patrol comes," she said.

Olivia darted inside. Zemanni followed. His scrutinizing glance roved over the space, his brow furrowing. It was another hangar bay. A much, much smaller one, but still... A large half-circle was cut out of the white flooring, revealing dark water beneath. The room wasn't as brightly lit as the hallways or the other hangar, the aqua crystal of the walls being the primary source of illumination. Unease trickled down Olivia's spine at the thought of the depths surrounding them.

"I thought you were taking us to Bron," she said.

The door slid shut behind them with a soft hush. The hairs on the nape of her neck stood on end. She turned around, her heart racing for reasons she didn't understand.

"Iridia?" she said.

"This is but a brief stop." Their guide stepped forward, her eyelids closing sideways over her aqua eyes. Her skin pulsed with a momentary wave of bioluminescence. Didn't that mean she was experiencing powerful emotion? Maybe she was taking a bigger risk than Olivia realized by bringing them here. She cringed inwardly as she thought of how much danger she had exposed Zemanni to without realizing it.

"Are you alright?" she asked.

"Yes." Iridia crossed to the interior wall of the hangar and opened another door. "But the patrols are coming. We need to hide here for a few minutes before it's clear to reach Bron."

Olivia hurried after her, stepping into the small room beyond. It looked like some sort of mechanical closet, with pipes and tubes running up and down along the walls. Blinking lights set between them might have been control buttons, but Olivia had no idea what they did.

"Come on," Iridia said, waving toward Zemanni.

He approached, but paused outside of the room, standing next to the Psiarae.

"Something's not right," he said.

Iridia let out a sigh and shook her head. "You always ruin everything."

What was she talking about? Before Olivia could ask, Iridia spun around so fast that she blurred, her right arm rising and gleaming in the light. Without pause, she rammed her fist through Zemanni's chest.

Olivia screamed, the sound echoing in the room. Iridia caught Zemanni against her slight frame, carrying him over the threshold into the mechanical closet. She rammed him against the back wall, pinning him there with an arm that suddenly looked more like a sword. Something in the wall behind Zemanni burst, and a stream of water started flowing to the floor. Zemanni let out a pained grunt, his eyes wide with shock as he stared at Iridia.

"What are you doing?" Olivia yelled, finally finding her voice.

Iridia turned to her and smiled, her pale, bluish-green skin turning pink. The silver coating her arm spread up and over her body, as if she was made of liquid mercury. The silver faded, leaving Olivia staring at a tall, thin man with tousled brown hair, wearing dark slacks and a black turtleneck. His eyes stayed silver, even the sclera.

Dean. Oh god, it's Dean.

They had all been warned about the Scorpiian. No one knew the extent of his powers, only that he'd been modified to give him abilities beyond those of any other shapeshifter from his homeworld. What she did know was that he was behind the kidnapping of Olivia's friend, Lian, and Craig and Barbara's new baby Lyrian. Dean had targeted the Cygnians, trying to manipulate their people into a war they wanted no part of. It was Dean's lockbox that had injured Bron. Dean was the reason she and Bron were here in the first place. The reason she had asked Zemanni to bring her to Ceres and then herself and Bron to this planet. And now, that favor might cost Zemanni his life.

"Please," Olivia pleaded.

"Begging already," Dean said in a breathy voice. "And I'm only getting started."

His expression darkened, his eyebrows pulling together, eyes narrowing as they turned to a chestnut brown. The muscles along his jaw jumped as he ground his teeth together. He turned back to Zemanni, and Dean's features contorted into absolute rage. Olivia had never seen so much anger. Her heart pounded painfully. She could barely breathe.

Zemanni stared up at Dean, eyes wide. Her friend's mouth opened and closed as if he was trying to speak, but nothing came out except a thin line of silver fluid. Zemanni clung to Dean's arms, as if his legs weren't strong enough to support him. Dean sneered and twisted his arm, pushing Zemanni higher.

Another scream escaped Olivia as Zemanni's feet lifted off the floor. He made a terrible choking sound, quicksilver flowing from his mouth. The scars around his neck and on his arms seeped more of the fluid, the jagged lines glowing brightly. Beneath his jeans and shirt, she could see more scars lighting up, the fabric becoming damp and sticking to his skin. Dean leaned closer, scrutinizing Zemanni's face.

"The great Zemanni." Dean bit out the words, his voice thick with contempt. "You were the most feared assassin in the galaxy. Now, look at you. Trapped in this form." Dean's lips curled away from his teeth. His arms were shaking. "You're pathetic."

Zemanni closed his eyes and more silver escaped them, running down his cheeks like tears. When he looked at Dean again, his fear and shock were gone. He looked as if he was trying to say something again, but Dean jostled the arm that was embedded in Zemanni's chest. All that came out was a gurgling grunt.

Olivia covered her mouth to stifle another scream. There was no one near enough to hear her. Not her voice. She placed her other hand over her heart, reaching out to Bron, begging him to sense her danger. She had wanted to help Bron handle whatever he was going through, but what she was facing… How could she get herself and Zemanni out of this? Had they sedated Bron to do their work? Was their bond strong enough for him to realize how much she needed him?

"You left me," Dean said. For a moment, his expression transformed. The rage vanished as a crushing despair entered his features, the stark vulnerability there making him seem much younger. "How could you leave me alone? With *them*?"

More quicksilver flowed from Zemanni's eyes. He slid one hand from Dean's arm to his shoulder, the movement costing him in pain that was written on his face. Dean lowered his head, then shook it, the anger returning in force. He lifted Zemanni higher still, his arm penetrating deeper into Zemanni's chest.

"You have these humans fooled," Dean said, his voice shaking with rage. "They think you care about them. As if you can care about anyone but yourself. Dressed in a borrowed skin. Have they ever seen what you really look like?" Dean glanced at Olivia. "I wonder if they'd care about you as much if you were trapped in a less familiar form."

He turned back to Zemanni, then closed his eyes tight. Dean's lips pinched together, and he drew in deep breaths through his nose. His arms glowed with a bright silver light that flowed into Zemanni's body.

"Please, don't." Olivia took a step forward, but Zemanni managed to look at her and shake his head brusquely. Silver flowed over his eyes before they rolled back in his head.

"Stop!" She screamed again as the light intensified, flowing through both men's bodies.

Zemanni's limbs and torso extended, his head becoming larger and rounder and his neck lengthening. His hair vanished and his eyes grew huge as his nose shrank against his face and his lips thinned. His clothing seemed voluminous around his thin body and his skin faded to a dull gray. The light dimmed, leaving her staring at Zemanni's true form—a Gray. He turned his head toward her, blinking his all-black eyes and opening the small slit of his mouth. His chest heaved in labored breaths.

"What do you want?" she yelled. Her voice shook as much as the rest of her.

Dean glanced over at her and smiled. He let Zemanni slowly sink along the wall to the floor, still stabbing the other Scorpiian through his chest. When Zemanni was crumpled against the wall, Dean finally pulled his arm out, the blade-like silver appendage transforming back to a normal human arm. He stepped away, sneering as Olivia threw herself forward to kneel at her friend's side. The cold water running over the floor of the room splashed against her, but didn't wet her clothing thanks to the Cygnian shielding around her.

Zemanni leaned against the wall, his eyes clenched shut and his mouth open as he pulled in breath after breath. Quicksilver seeped from his old wounds and the new one. She couldn't imagine the agony he had endured when he had pulled himself back together using his shapeshifting ability, or the pain he must be feeling now that those wounds were reopening.

"What do I do?" she asked, reaching toward him with shaking hands. His skin was smooth and cold. The texture had an odd give to it that made her hesitate to put pressure anywhere, but at least she could give him the comfort of her touch.

"You watch him die," Dean said. "But don't worry. You'll join him soon enough." He tapped his foot in the water.

Her heart clenched with terror. She knew Dean could make good on his threat, that he would kill her or let her drown. But she still didn't know why.

She sniffed and shook her head. "Why are you doing this?"

"Why does anyone do terrible things?" he said. "For love."

Dean frowned, the rage dissipating as he seemed to stare through her. He glanced over at Zemanni and some of the color drained from his face. Dean was so good at pretending to be human. He almost looked sorry. His expression hardened once more, his lips tightening into a thin line. He turned and opened the door. He was halfway through when Zemanni lifted a long, gangly arm toward him.

"Zakarri," he said, his voice high and with an odd reverberation to it.

Dean froze, his shoulders rising as he hunched in the doorway, one hand on the frame. His knuckles went bloodless from his grip.

"I'm sorry." Zemanni's hand dropped to his side,

splashing in the deepening water.

Dean looked back at him, his lips parted and features pinched with such pain, Olivia would be haunted by it forever. His eyes flooded with silver. He closed them tight, taking in a deep breath and letting it out. A line of silver leaked from his eye, but was quickly reabsorbed by his skin. When he looked at them again, his gaze was the same brown it had been before.

For a moment, she thought he might turn back to them. He seemed torn. Perhaps he really felt regret. But then he turned away and was gone, the door sliding shut behind him, throwing them into near-darkness.

A sob wracked her as she lifted Zemanni's hand and held it in hers. His body put off a soft silver light, just enough for her to see his features. He angled his head toward her, his mouth moving as if he was trying to speak.

"Save your strength," she said, forcing a smile through her tears. She gently stroked his head, squeezing his hand as tightly as she dared. "You're going to be fine."

He closed his eyes, his mouth clamping shut. His breaths were slowing. Quicksilver spread out around them in a mirrorlike pool, floating on the surface of the rising water. How much could he lose before he…

She shook the thought away. He was going to be okay. They all were.

"Bron is going to reach us," she said. "He'll save us. Please, you can't give up. Not when it's my fault you're here."

Zemanni's brow ridge furrowed between his eyes as he looked at her again. He lifted his free hand slightly, then let out a gasping sigh. His hand fell as his head listed against his shoulder. Olivia leaned forward, cradling his head against her chest, tears coursing over her cheeks.

"Please, Bron," she murmured. "We need you."

Chapter Eighteen

Once more, Bron lay on one of the Psiaraen operating tables, staring up at the bubbles moving slowly through clear pipes filled with a liquid that put off aqua light. His agitation rose. At least this time, he was clothed, though they had cut off the bottom of the left leg of his pants. Two Psiarae hovered above him, both female this time. He recognized Tethis now as the woman who had originally helped him.

"Where is the male?" Bron asked.

"What male?" Tethis said.

"The one who assisted you before. Where is he?"

She turned to him, lips pinched and eyes tight. "He has left us."

Did that mean he had left the city or had he passed on? Either way, from the pain on her features, he was certain it had been a blow. Bron paused for a few moments, then said, "I'm sorry for your loss."

She didn't reply, but returned her attention to his leg. "The Scorpiian did not merely poison the trap on his lockbox. He also injected you with nanites."

Bron's stomach clenched. How many exposures to

various nanites had he undergone at this point? The Psiarae's, Norem's formula, now Dean?

"Why didn't your nanites deactivate them?"

"They could not do so," she said. "You have been host to a war ever since you were damaged. It is astounding that you fared well enough to make it to us."

That was dangerously close to a compliment. Rather than bring attention to it, he said, "Are you able to send in reinforcements?"

She turned to stare at him.

"It's an Earth expression," he said. "When their battles were going poorly, they would send in reinforcements."

"That is an interesting idea. We were planning to initiate a system purge, after which we would install a new set of nanites."

Bron's hearts beat faster. That would take time and would incapacitate him. The pain he could endure. Leaving Olivia to fend for herself for that long was unacceptable.

"I need to return to Olivia," he said.

"We understand your soulmate bonds." Tethis's lip curled up slightly as she spoke. "But there are protocols to follow." She turned back to his leg, attaching various mechanisms to it.

Protocols. The Cygnians had protocols of their own. Because of them, Lar had nearly died—no, he had *actually* died. If it hadn't been for the primitive Earth medical techniques that Becca and Sophie insisted they employ, they wouldn't have been able to bring him back.

Bron wondered if there were any Earth techniques that might help him. He accessed the databanks within the cybernetic cortex the nanites had built in his brain, where he had downloaded various methodologies. One immediately presented itself as a viable possibility.

"Draw them out," Bron said.

"What?" Tethis didn't look up from her work.

"When Earthlings are poisoned, they sometimes use suction to draw out the toxin or venom."

This time, Tethis stopped. She arched an eyebrow at him, a flash of something that almost looked like amusement crossing her features.

"You want us to suck the nanites out of your leg?" she asked.

"It's more complicated than that," he said. "But perhaps you can lure them out somehow. Or the nanites within me can be programmed to drive them out somehow. And if you can collect them, you can study them more fully."

She pursed her lips. "An interesting concept."

She turned to her assistant and began a long line of trilling sounds. The other Psiarae nodded, then crossed the room to gather some things. While she was gone, Tethis shifted her weight uneasily.

"I will allow you to leave," she said.

"What?"

"You are intelligent. No doubt, you have been wondering whether I would allow you to leave after having brought outsiders to our planet. But you are an outsider yourself. I do not want you here. *We* do not want you here."

"I understand."

"We will increase our planetary defenses. You will not be able to return."

"I wouldn't have come if it wasn't a matter of life and death."

She nodded. "All sentients have a will to survive."

"I would have died to protect your secret," Bron said. "And I will continue to protect it as best I can. But Olivia and I are bonded. If I die, she dies. I can't let that happen."

Tethis was silent for a moment, then nodded again. The other Psiarae appeared at her side, holding a small metal cylinder. Bron watched the hologram that hovered above him, mirroring his body, with open interest this time. They attached the cylinder to the injury on his leg, then placed small cubes filled with millions of glowing lights at his neck and near his injury. Nanite injectors.

"You will need to program them once they are inside of you," Tethis said. "Are you ready?"

"I am."

Tethis nodded to her assistant. A soft hiss accompanied the deployment of the nanites into his system.

There was no pain this time, only that odd chill as his body once more became home to new technology. The nanites began interfacing with his systems, replicating the commands he had given to his existing supply. The best option seemed to be targeted EMP bursts. Any invading nanites caught in the field would be deactivated. Those evading the bursts would be herded back to the injury site, where the cylinder would collect them.

There was risk. Electromagnetic pulses could damage his systems. But Bron didn't have time to waste. He could sense Olivia's agitation. She wanted to be with him. They needed to be together.

His skin rippled with odd tingling sensations as his cybernetic senses fed him data that his Cygnian nerves tried to understand. His nanites pushed forward, their reinforcements traveling closely behind them and repairing the collateral damage from the EMPs. Now, the pain came, but he kept it at bay, focusing on pushing every single invading nanite from his body. Tethis and her assistant watched the holodisplay intently, their wide eyes never blinking.

Finally, Bron felt the last of Dean's nanites leave his body. The remaining nanites—his own nanites—immediately began repairing other systems that had been compromised during their invasion. The static that had been plaguing him vanished.

"Extraordinary," Tethis said. "We must run more tests."

"Later," Bron said. "I need to return to Olivia."

"In time." Tethis waved at him dismissively, staring at the hologram above him. "We must capture the data regarding how your body deals with this issue."

It made sense they should want to do so, and Bron didn't wish to deprive them of this data when they had helped him. At the same time, though he felt better physically, emotionally, he was worse. His agitation grew, his hearts beating faster and his claws extending from the fingertips of his right hand.

"Calm yourself," Tethis said. "You are corrupting our data."

"Something is wrong," Bron said.

"Your cybernetic systems are working within expected parameters," Tethis said. "Though there are oddities in your biological readings." She pointed at something on the blue side of the hologram, trilling to her assistant.

"Something is wrong with Olivia," Bron said. He could feel her unease rising.

"She is being guarded by a hundred of our best soldiers. She is fine."

"She is not."

A sharp burst of panic flooded his mind. Olivia was terrified, in shock. Something had happened. Something horrible. Bron leapt to his feet. The moment he was off the table, his spine plates snapped up, their vibration strong enough to disrupt the holographic display. Panic flooded him.

"You cannot leave," Tethis said. "We have not finished collecting data. You are not fully repaired."

"Make do with what data you have." He headed toward the door, but staggered as a wave of dizziness assailed him. He sucked in a breath. The air tasted strange on his tongue. Salty and filled with an odd floral tinge. The lights stung his eyes and his neck ached.

"We are still scanning your biological systems," she said. "You have been exposed to some sort of genetic pathogen."

"Later," he said, willing the room to right itself.

"Where are you even—" Before Tethis could finish her question, the hologram above the table morphed into a face that had Bron's hearts pounding. A face he recognized.

"Dean," Bron said.

"Hello, Cygnian," Dean said.

"What is the meaning of this?" Tethis demanded.

Dean cocked his head to the side as he looked at her. "I would say this doesn't concern you, but it does. Now shut up and do exactly as I say."

Tethis's chest expanded, as if she was about to light into Dean, but before she could speak, Dean's features rippled and changed, his eyes growing wider and his features more delicate.

"Iridia…" Tethis gasped.

"Mom..." Iridia's voice shook with fear. She glanced around as if terrified. "Mom, you need to do what he says. I'm so scared."

"Iridia, I—"

"Oh, please." Iridia began to laugh, her features relaxing.

The hologram rippled again, but this time, Bron realized it wasn't the display changing. It was Dean's face.

"Too easy," Dean said.

Tethis's eyes blinked sideways, her mouth slack. She trilled for a few moments, the sound disjointed, as if she wasn't sure what to say. Then her features darkened with rage.

"If you hurt my daughter, there will be no corner of this universe where you will be safe," she said.

"If I had a dime for every time I've heard that..." Dean said. "Well, I'd be even richer than I am."

"What do you want, Dean?" Bron asked, trying to mask his own panic from his voice. Olivia was being guarded by a hundred Psiaraen soldiers. Surely she was safe with them. But if that was so, why did he sense so much fear from her?

"What do I want?" Dean glared at Bron. "What I want, you can't give me. But you can help me get it."

"I can arrange for your lockbox to be returned," Bron said.

Dean laughed. "I don't give a crap about the lockbox.

Keep it. What I want from you is more personal. So, let's discuss it. Just you and me."

"But, my daughter..." Tethis said.

"Will be fine," Dean said. "As long as Bron cooperates. He knows where to find me. Send anyone else and more people suffer. A lot more."

More? Who was already hurt? Bron's spine plates sent out a warning pulse as their vibration increased.

Dean looked at Bron and said, "I don't know that much about your Cygnian technology yet, but I do know it tends to run out of power in darkness. You might want to hurry." The hologram disappeared.

Tethis turned to him, her eyes pleading. Bron nodded, then ran for the door.

Olivia's fear was a beacon. Bron sprinted down corridor after corridor, finally stopping in front of an open door that led into a small hangar bay. He stepped inside cautiously. Dean was leaning against a small vessel that floated just above the water, his arms and ankles crossed in a pose that was oddly similar to the way Zemanni had stood on the bridge of his ship earlier.

Dean's ship looked like a mix between Scorpiian and Centauran technology. Bron's stomach lurched. Centaurans had new cloaking technology that no one could penetrate yet, not even the Vegans. If Olivia was on that ship and Dean left with her, Bron would have only their link to find her again.

"Where are Olivia and Iridia?" Bron demanded.

"What, no concern for Zemanni?" Dean shook his head. "That's cold."

Bron remained silent, though he realized with some surprise that he was concerned for the other Scorpiian.

"It's just as well," Dean said. "I don't think he's going to make it. But hey, he had a good run."

Bron's hearts stuttered. Zemanni might not be what Bron would call a friend, but Olivia saw him as such. And Zemanni had brought them both here. He had barely complained when Bron had taken control of his ship. Bron's spine plates vibrated more strongly. His feet widened into a fighting stance.

Dean only laughed.

"Didn't your big bro tell you what happened when he tried to fight me back on *Outreach* station?" Dean shook his head. "As much as I'd love to see the look on your face if I reenacted that fight, I'm pressed for time. Actually, you're pressed for time."

Dean glanced over at a door to one side of the hangar. The floor in front of it reflected the light oddly. Bron took a step closer, his feet splashing in water that flowed from beneath it.

"Olivia," he yelled, running forward.

"You won't be able to open it," Dean said. "Not even with your quaint little nanites."

Bron ignored him, pounding on the door. "Olivia!" he

yelled again.

He heard her muffled cry in response, relief and love flowing out from her. He had to hold her in his arms, but the damned door wouldn't give. Bron slammed his cybernetic hand on the control panel next to it, blasting it with commands to open. His nanites returned a steady stream of bizarre data, the encryption changing so rapidly, it would take him hours to work through it.

"Relax," Dean said. "I'll open it for you. If you play nice."

"What do you want, Scorpiian?" Bron said.

"Simple." Dean shrugged one shoulder. "I want you."

Chapter Nineteen

The light Zemanni was putting off grew dimmer with each moment. Olivia held him close, trying to figure out what to do when the water level rose high enough to cover his nose. Would it hurt him for her to lift him up? Could Scorpiians drown? The water had been rising steadily and was already up to his chest. She had sensed Bron outside, heard him banging on the door, but then he had stopped. A feeling of calm determination had overwhelmed everything else coming from him, aside from the love he felt for her.

Now, she was alone in the near dark, and she could tell he was getting farther away. She couldn't imagine what would have made him leave her. She didn't want to. All she could do was focus on where she was and how to help her friend.

A crack of light appeared around the door. Olivia's heart leapt to her throat. The door opened, letting the water rush outside—and taking Zemanni's quicksilver with it.

"No, no, no," she said, reaching out and trying to scoop as much of the liquid into her arms as she could.

She heard a gasp and looked over to see Iridia standing

in the open doorway. Her skin was paler than before and, beneath her jaw, her gills opened and closed almost frantically. Iridia saw what Olivia was doing and dropped to her knees, blocking as much of the silver fluid from draining away as she could.

"Are you alright?" she asked, without looking up from her work.

"No," Olivia moaned. "Zemanni..."

Iridia glanced up. "I see that your friend is injured, but are *you* alright? I need to know."

"I'm... I don't know. Physically, I'm fine. But something is happening with Bron. Something terrible."

"Where is he?"

"I'm not sure."

Olivia sniffed, then ran her hand over Zemanni's forehead. He was so still. She didn't know enough about Scorpiian anatomy to tell if... if... She shook her head. Thinking like that wouldn't help, and she wasn't giving up on anyone until she had to.

"I think..." Her voice shook. "I think Dean took him."

"The other Scorpiian?" Iridia's skin began to strobe. Olivia quickly looked away so that it wouldn't mesmerize her again.

"Yes," Olivia said. She had a peaceful nature, but if she ever saw Dean again, she wasn't sure what she'd do.

Zemanni roused a bit, but then his head listed to the side again. Olivia's stomach lurched. He was alive! Her heart pounded painfully, its quick beat making her dizzy. It was hard to catch her breath.

Iridia looked at the quicksilver pooled on the floor around them, her mouth set in a grim line. She reached up and pulled off her collar. A long, flexible tube was attached to the back of it, hidden beneath her hair. She detached a small cylinder from her belt that was at the other end of the tube and set it on the floor in front of her.

"Don't you need that to breathe?" Olivia asked, alarmed.

"I can survive for some time without it. Your friend is in greater danger."

She began adjusting the mechanism, pouring out the liquid it held. She disconnected the tube, then held it to the quicksilver. At the press of a button, it started drawing the fluid up into the cylinder. It seemed to take forever, but eventually, there was no gleaming silver on the floor. Zemanni's wound still leaked a steady stream.

"We must get him to my mother," Iridia said. "She'll know what to do."

Olivia nodded, then pulled one of Zemanni's arms over her shoulder. Iridia did the same on his other side. He was lighter than Olivia expected, and the pair maneuvered him out of the hangar bay and down the corridors Iridia led them through.

"This is the main laboratory and medical bay used for air-breathers," Iridia said, stopping before a door. "We can contact my mother once we're inside." She reached up to the control panel next to the door and it slid open.

"Or... not," Olivia said.

Tethis paced inside the room. When the door opened, she stopped and turned to them, her eyes wide with shock. Instead of running toward them, she stepped back and pointed.

"Guards," she shouted.

"Mother, wait," Iridia yelled back. "It's me."

Tethis shook her head. "How... How can I be certain?"

"Mother..." Iridia said.

It wasn't a giant leap for Olivia to realize that Dean must have taken Iridia's form to get to Bron. She had never hated anyone before, but Dean...

"Dean left," Olivia said. "The other Scorpiian. He—" Her voice broke. "He got what he came for."

"Please, mother." Iridia started dragging them toward one of the medical beds. "You must help Zemanni."

"I am finished helping outsiders," Tethis said. "Iridia, get away from that thing."

"Zemanni did nothing wrong," Olivia said. "Please, he's dying."

"That is not our concern," Tethis said.

Olivia was desperate for a way to convince Tethis to help. She didn't know how to save Zemanni and doubted Iridia had the knowledge to do so, either. But maybe... Maybe Zemanni did.

"He knows Dean," Olivia said. "Zemanni knows the other Scorpiian. If you let him die, you'll never know who you're dealing with or if he plans to return."

"Mother..." Iridia begged.

Tethis glared at Olivia, then turned her stony gaze on Zemanni. After what felt like an eternity, she shook her head and motioned toward one of the beds. Olivia and Iridia carried Zemanni to it, helping him to lie down.

"I will do what I can for this Scorpiian," Tethis said. "But after we interrogate him, you will all leave and never return."

"That's fine." Olivia would be happy never to return to this place. She felt bad for Iridia, but all Olivia wanted was to find where Dean had taken Bron.

She stepped back as Iridia handed the cylinder full of quicksilver to Tethis. Another Psiarae approached Iridia and handed her a new collar and cylinder. She put them on, stringing the tube down her back. When she was done, she joined Olivia against the wall, watching as Tethis went to work on Zemanni.

"If anyone can save him, my mother can," Iridia whispered.

Olivia nodded, trying not to think of how similar this situation felt to what she'd experienced after her accident. Seeing the table surrounded by people doing their best to patch Zemanni back together... She turned away, hugging herself tight. She'd done all she could for her friend. Now, all she could think about was Bron.

"How long do you think it will take?" Olivia asked.

"I'm not sure. He is grievously injured."

Tears streaked down Olivia's face. "I have to get to Bron. I can still feel him close by."

"Are you sure that—"

"He's alive," Olivia said. "I would know if he... If something had happened."

But something *was* happening. He was terrified, and it went beyond his fear for her.

"He isn't in the city," Olivia said.

"His wristbands will enable him to survive in the ocean for some time. We'll mount a search party as soon as—"

Olivia's mouth went dry. "He isn't wearing wristbands. He gave his to me to keep me safe." And now, he was out there alone, with no way to survive the harsh conditions of this planet.

"I have studied the soulmate phenomenon in Cygnians." Iridia found Olivia's hand and squeezed it. "As long as you can sense him, there is still hope."

'I will always find my way back to you.'

Bron's words echoed in her mind. Olivia prayed he was right. But she wasn't about to just stand around and wait for him to find his way back. Not when she could sense that he was in danger.

"Can we trust your mother with Zemanni?" Olivia whispered.

"Yes."

"Then come on. I need your help."

Chapter Twenty

Bron sat against the bulkhead of Dean's ship, trying desperately to figure out what to do. He had already tried to link up with the ship's systems, but the computer was more advanced than anything Bron had encountered before. He recognized Centauran aspects to it, as well as Scorpiian signatures, but there was another distinct technology woven through that was almost Vegan, yet even more advanced.

The Coalition was in greater danger than they realized —as was Earth. If the Tau Centauran Assembly had access to this advanced technology, it was only a matter of time before they would take over the entire galaxy. Bron wanted to warn them, to help, but he couldn't even help himself.

The Scorpiian had left him in the airlock, with only an energy field between Bron and the dark waters of Gamma Piscium 1. No doubt, it was a reminder of what would happen if Bron tried to escape. There was nowhere for him to go, and if he damaged the ship, he would likely drown. The thought of sinking to the bottom of the ocean surrounding him sent a chill down his spine plates.

The only thing keeping him from absolute panic was knowing that Olivia was unharmed. Physically, at least. She was distraught—worried both for Bron and Zemanni. Bron had seen the trace of quicksilver in the water seeping from under the door where she was held prisoner.

When Dean had ordered him to go with him, Bron had seen no other choice. At least he'd been right in trusting Dean to let Olivia go. Her fear had shifted after they left, from the immediate panic of facing drowning that he fought now to a broader fear that she wouldn't be able to save those she loved.

Maker, he loved how much she cared for others. Bonding with her, feeling what was in her heart, had been the best experience of his life. He only hoped that it wouldn't mean the end of hers. He didn't know what Dean intended to do with him. Bron only knew that he had to survive. He had to return to Olivia. The light of Psiaraht grew smaller as they headed toward the ocean's surface. Once they left the planet, Bron would have the icy void of space to contend with. He wasn't seeing many options.

Movement in the hallway caught his attention. Dean strode up to the other side of the transparent airlock door, looking down at Bron through its clear paneling. It would be so easy for Bron to crash through it. But then, Dean could just drop the energy field keeping the water at bay. This was the Psiaraen homeworld. They could survive and traverse their oceans just fine, and Dean could take their form. But Bron would sink like the stones of his own homeworld.

Dean leaned against the wall opposite the door, his hands in his pockets and a grim frown on his face. Strange. Bron would have thought he'd be happy to have his quarry.

"It's nothing personal, you know," Dean said.

"What? You attacking my soulmate and taking me prisoner?"

"Well..." Dean shrugged. "Yeah."

Bron snorted and shook his head. "What about Zemanni? You Scorpiians are a competitive bunch, I've heard."

Dean looked away. A muscle stood out in his jaw as he ground his teeth together. Finally, he turned his gaze downward.

"Yeah, that's... That part's personal," Dean said. "But the rest of it—you and Olivia, even that Psiaraen princess —that's all just... a means to an end."

"And what end is that?"

Dean's lips pulled into an odd smirk. "Love."

"You're not my type," Bron said.

Dean laughed. "Yeah, well, you're not mine either. But Hayley is."

"Hayley?" Bron knew that name.

Hayley was a friend of Becca, Sophie, and Amy, the three Earthling sisters who were the soulmates of Lar,

Karl, and Bron's brother, Dorn. Dean had abducted Hayley, then handed her over to Norem. From what Bron knew, Dean had meant to return for her, but something about her fascinated Norem, and the Tau Ceti scientist had run off with the unfortunate Earthling for his studies. The only comfort they had was knowing that Hayley had gone along with Norem willingly.

Tobek had told them he and Hayley made a deal where she would try to find one of Tobek's friends that Norem had sent to another base in exchange for Tobek guarding the three sisters. If it hadn't been for Tobek's help, at least two of the sisters would have been killed. Even with his intervention, Amy had nearly died. Hayley was as close as family with the sisters. Bron was certain that wherever she was, she would be grateful that her sacrifice had protected them.

"Hayley is my soulmate," Dean said.

Bron stared at him for a moment, then laughed. Dean's brow lowered over his eyes and his mouth pulled into a deep scowl.

"Hayley was so repulsed by you that she chose Norem's lab over your arms." Bron laughed again.

"She was frightened and confused," Dean said.

"Yes, so confused that she was able to negotiate a partnership with one of her captors that ended up saving the lives of those dearest to her."

Dean's glare intensified. He pushed himself off from

the wall and pressed his hand against the control panel next to the airlock. Bron rose to his feet, squaring off with the Scorpiian through the transparent door.

"And to think I felt bad for you," Dean said. "Thanks for helping with that."

"What do you mean?"

Dean's eyes flooded with silver, his hand morphing to fuse with the controls. Something cold and wet seeped around Bron's feet. He looked down to see water flowing in through the airlock's outer door. The energy field still held, trapping him inside, but water flowed through it in greater and greater amounts, pouring down its inner surface.

"What are you doing?" Bron yelled, pressing himself against the inner door.

"I told you I needed you to come with me," Dean said. "I never said I needed you alive."

The water was already up to Bron's knees and rising fast. He pounded on the transparent plane of the airlock door. Bright motes of light sparked out with each impact. Another energy field. Bron was trapped. He tried to link up with the ship's computer again, but his nanites couldn't manage the interface.

"I'll be back in a few minutes," Dean said. "It should be over then." He turned and walked out of sight down the corridor.

Bron pounded on the door again, to no avail. The water

was up to his waist. He looked around, trying to find anything that might help. Any way to escape. There was nothing. He was going to drown, and then Dean could use the technology in Bron's body for whatever foul plans he was working on. He could help the Assembly gain even more power.

Bron's hearts raced as his mind scrolled through scenarios, each more terrifying than the one before. What could he do to stop this? He took deep, calming breaths, pulling his mind back to reason, thinking through his options. The only thing that presented itself was death.

If he died, Olivia would die, too. Surely there was something he could do to save them both? When he opened his eyes again, he was facing the outer door of the airlock. Water streamed in, up to his chest now. The cold didn't bother him so much as the knowledge that it would soon fill the entire chamber.

Bron calmed himself further. He didn't want Olivia to feel his fear. If this was the end, he wouldn't make it harder for either of them. The water rose to his chin. He tilted his head back, unable to bring his body any higher. There was nothing to climb, and he was too dense to float.

He closed his eyes and thought of his soulmate. Of her warm eyes and radiant smile. Of the loving, tender heart that beat within her breast.

His breathing calmed further, his hearts slowing. The water was nearly to his nose, but the fear he'd been fighting was gone. A wave of calm ease flowed through his body, cooling him and washing away the last of the strange fever he'd experienced on the journey to Gamma Piscium 1.

His chest felt strangely full. He opened his eyes and let out a yell when he saw that the water had already filled the chamber. A few bubbles escaped his mouth—the last of his breath. In a panic, he sucked in a lungful of water.

More coolness. More ease.

He exhaled. The current of the water leaving his body tickled across his cheek and neck. Reaching up, he felt strange flaps beneath his jaw and along both sides of his neck. Gills?

He thought back to the tanks that had held the Tau Ceti that Norem was experimenting on. They had been floating in a serum meant to alter their DNA—to add Cygnian elements to their fundamental makeup. Had Bron been changed by it as well, after such a short exposure? Had the Tau Ceti DNA somehow made its way into him?

He took another breath, pulling water into his lungs. Aside from a slight dizziness, he felt fine. Perhaps too fine. Dean might be watching. Waiting for Bron to 'die.' He would happily oblige the Scorpiian. Bron shook his limbs and body, pretending to struggle, then let himself fall to his knees, propped against a wall. When Dean opened the door, Bron would be ready. He only hoped Dean wouldn't just leave Bron as he was until they reached whatever destination Dean had in mind.

The extra weight of the water in the airlock would make exiting the atmosphere more difficult. It was more reasonable to empty the airlock before trying to leave the planet. Minutes dragged by as Bron waited. Finally, his hopes were answered as a vibration began beneath the floor. Pumps siphoned off the water, expelling it from the ship. Bron did his best to time his release of the water held in his lungs. The air burned at first when he slowly inhaled again, but he kept his body still. The door to the airlock opened.

Bron was on his feet instantly, lashing out to grab Dean by the neck and slam the Scorpiian against the wall opposite the airlock. For a glorious moment, Dean's eyes were wide with shock, his mouth slack. Bron didn't dare give him time to recover. He twisted his hand, snapping Dean's neck. Dean's brows lowered as he snarled. Bron might have… miscalculated.

Pressing his hands to Bron's chest, Dean shoved him so hard that he flew back into the airlock. The transparent door slid back into place. Bron leapt forward, smashing his hand through it door before Dean could get the interior energy field back up. Bron grabbed the metal frame of the door and tore it from its moorings, flinging it aside. Impossibly powerful hands latched onto his shoulders, pulling him back into the corridor. His momentum didn't stop until his head smashed into the wall. Pain screamed along his spine from the impact.

Bron fell back from the wall, staggering and shaking his head to clear it. A dent marred the smooth surface of the wall at least a foot deep. How was Dean so strong? Bron wheeled around, looking for his opponent, but the corridor was empty. The briefest hint of movement was his only warning before Dean dropped on him from the ceiling, locking his arms around Bron's neck.

"I don't think Norem needs your head to be attached to study you," Dean said. "I can still trade you for Hayley."

Bron turned and slammed Dean into the wall with all his might, over and over again, hard enough to add several more dents to the metal. The Scorpiian's hold only tightened. Dean clawed at Bron's head, tilting it at a painful angle. His spine popped as the vertebrae began to separate.

If Bron couldn't hurt Dean, he could use Dean to hurt his ship. He turned and slammed Dean against the control panel next to the airlock. A crackling alarm sounded as it shorted out. The energy field on the outer door failed. Water poured into the corridor. Bron almost smiled at its welcome arrival. He grabbed the sides of the inner door and pulled himself into the airlock, fighting the current.

"What are you doing?" Dean shouted, no longer trying to rip Bron's head from his shoulders.

Bron laughed. "Going for a swim."

He pulled himself out of the ship, but kept his grip on

one of the protruding edges of the hull. Dean released him, letting the water push him back inside. Bron didn't dare let himself rest for a moment. He crawled up the ship, using whatever handhold he could find. Every time he saw something that looked vulnerable to his strength, he broke it. He maneuvered himself to one of the viewports and started slamming his fist against it until cracks snaked through its surface.

The ship rolled suddenly, its belly momentarily facing up as it did a full rotation. Bron's grip slipped. He flailed his arms and legs, but it was no use. The gravity of the planet pulled him down into the inky depths. The last bit of light Bron saw was Dean's ship firing its thrusters to break through the planet's icy surface.

Chapter Twenty-One

"Are you certain he's still alive?" Iridia asked, for what seemed the hundredth time.

"Yes, I'm sure." Olivia bit her lip as she stared out the front viewport of the water shuttle that they had stolen and used to leave the city. The ship's computer was enhancing the images of what surrounded them, casting everything in a haunting purple glow. An image of the ocean floor dominated the view, each surface outlined in grids to make it easier for her to see features like mountains and valleys. The sheer enormity of it was almost overwhelming. But she wouldn't give up. She would never give up.

"It's been hours," Iridia said. "Why wouldn't Dean have taken him offworld by now?"

Olivia shook her head. "I don't know. I just know that he's in front of us and... down."

Iridia sighed, but a few moments later, the ship descended further. They were so close to the ocean floor she had to steer around boulders the size of buildings.

"Without his wristbands—" Iridia began.

Olivia flailed an arm at her and said, "Shh. What is that?"

She stepped closer to the screen, pointing at an oddly shaped rock. An oddly shaped rock moving in their direction. The ship projected a beam of light, illuminating the blue-skinned figure before them.

"What in the..." Iridia's voice trailed off.

"It's him. It's Bron." Olivia could barely believe it herself, but there he was, walking along the bottom of the ocean, heading right for them, one hand held up to shield his eyes from the ship's light.

"This isn't possible," Iridia said. "I thought you told me he didn't have wristbands to provide him with atmosphere."

"I did. I mean, he doesn't. I don't know what's going on, but we have to get to him. How do we get to him?"

"Don't worry, there's a pressurized chamber with a water entrance that we use to come and go when we're making trips outside of the city with cargo that requires air."

Bron stopped, staring up at their ship. His eyes were two pale pinpricks of light. Iridia piloted the ship directly above him.

"Why doesn't he swim to the hatch?" she asked.

"Cygnians can't swim," Olivia said. "They're too dense."

"He's just lucky their homeworld has a similar pressure to ours or he would've been squished."

Olivia blocked that thought from her brain. "Can you

get the ship closer?"

"I'll do my best."

On the screen, Olivia watched as the ship lowered closer to the ocean's floor. She couldn't breathe. Bron was so close. What had happened while they'd been separated?

The viewport flickered, then changed to show the underside of the ship. Bron ducked, then sort of shuffled to the side before gripping the edge of the hatch and pulling himself up. His legs disappeared into the ship. Olivia turned and ran from the bridge.

Down. She needed to go down to get to him. They had passed a ladder on their way to the bridge. She ran through a few short corridors until she found it. Her hands were slick against the metal as she hurried toward her soulmate. The skirt of her dress caught on a rung when she had just passed the ceiling of the bottom level of the ship.

"Dammit, why do I always wear these things?"

She reached down to pull it free, but it was really stuck. With one last giant tug, it came free, but she used so much force that her other hand slipped from the ladder. Screaming, she fell, only to be caught in muscular arms. She looked up into glowing blue eyes and a smiling face she had been afraid she'd never see again.

"Bron," she said. "You kept your promise. You found your way back to me."

"I will always find my way back to you. Especially if you come and pick me up when I'm only halfway there."

She laughed and smiled, tears flowing down her cheeks. "I will always come for you."

His smile turned wicked. "That is a promise I will delight in making you keep repeatedly."

He pressed his lips to hers in a kiss that curled her toes. The vibration of his spine plates resonated through her. She wrapped her arms around his neck, pulling him closer. She couldn't get him close enough. Bron shifted his grip, bringing her in front of him. She wrapped her legs around his waist as he pushed her skirt up to her waist.

This. This was why she always wore dresses. At least, it would be from now on. She was suddenly glad she hadn't had a chance to put her underwear back on before they'd left the base on Ceres.

Bron's tongue plunged into her mouth. The same desperation she felt flowed out from him. He walked them to the nearest wall, reaching between them to loosen the ties of his pants. The moment he pressed her back to the wall, his lower dick was at her core, driving in deep.

Her skin was on fire, tingling energy rocketing along her nerves. He held her legs in a tight grip as he drove himself into her over and over again. His upper cock slid along her clit with each stroke. Pleasure wracked her body, coiling around where they were connected until she exploded in a fiery burst of ecstasy that consumed all thought.

Bron kept his hold on her lips, groaning against them

as she felt him pulse deep within her. His hips kept moving, with barely a pause as he let his lower dick slide from her body and immediately impaled her with his primary. He swallowed her cries as she was stretched even farther, her sheath contracting around him in rhythmic aftershocks from her first orgasm.

His thrusts became almost frenzied, his hands squeezing her thighs, his chest pinning her to the wall. The echoes of her climax rekindled into a blaze. Her skin was on fire. Her muscles, her bones molten heat. She was only this passion, this incredible connection cascading through every part of her body. Her belly tightened, then exploded in waves of bliss, her core pulsing around him. He threw his head back and roared as he poured his seed into her, each stroke pushing her higher into her own climax.

Finally, he slowed his thrusts and then stopped, holding her against the wall. He kissed the side of her neck gently and grazed his teeth along her skin, sending shivers through her that promised so much more.

"I missed you, too," she said, in a breathless voice.

Bron slid from her body, then lowered her to her feet. She brushed her skirt down while he refastened his pants.

"We should let Iridia know you made it onboard," Olivia said.

"Oh, I'm aware." Iridia's voice sounded high and strained over the ship's communication systems.

"Oops." Olivia felt her cheeks heat. Still, she couldn't

stop smiling. "I think we might have taught her more than we intended about human-Cygnian mating practices."

"We must return to Earth as quickly as possible," Bron said, leaning in close. "Unless we wish to continue her lessons."

Olivia nodded, then turned toward the ladder. Bron followed closely as they climbed back to the main level and headed for the bridge.

"What of Zemanni?" Bron asked.

Olivia's heart gave a little tug that he had thought to ask. "We aren't sure yet. We've been keeping our communications silent. Iridia wasn't sure how her mother would feel about us running off to look for you."

They entered the bridge to find Iridia sitting in the command chair, her back ramrod straight. Her skin was flushed a bright aqua around her cheeks and her eyes were wide and unblinking.

Olivia leaned closer to Bron and said, "I think we traumatized her."

"She'll live." He chuckled, running his hand down along her back.

"Hello," Iridia said, too-brightly. "I'm glad you made it."

"Thank you," Bron said. "It would have been a long walk back to the city."

"How did you escape?" Iridia asked. "And what did that Scorpiian even want with you?"

Olivia sensed an odd pang of sympathy flow out from Bron. She turned to face him, openly curious.

"He wanted to trade me to a Tau Ceti scientist who has been working on perfecting Tau Cygnian cyborgs," Bron said.

Iridia's face paled. "That's awful. If he had obtained you..."

"It would not have been good for any of the sentients in the galaxy," Bron said.

"You can't tell my mother," Iridia said.

Olivia shook her head. "Iridia, we can't ask you to keep secrets for us. You've already done enough."

"No, if you tell her, she'll never let you leave," Iridia said. "She'll become even more paranoid and isolationist. We're already cut off from so much. The only Psiarae who get to see anything are the few sent to observe." She sucked in her breath as if trying to pull the words back into her.

"Dean will not get another chance to take me," Bron said, glossing over the information she had undoubtedly over-shared. "Now that we know I'm a target, we will take precautions. And I don't think he'll have the patience to try again."

"Why?" Olivia asked. "What was he going to trade you for?"

"Hayley," Bron said.

Chapter Twenty-Two

The trip to the city didn't take long. Iridia had already turned the shuttle around when she saw Bron was safely aboard and being... welcomed by Olivia. He couldn't wait to return to the *Arrow* and be 'welcomed' some more.

Iridia led them back to the medical bay. Zemanni was in a bed that had been propped up so that he had a better view of the room. His skin barely had more color than the sheets he rested on and a fine sheen of glowing sweat coated his brow. Olivia gasped when she saw him, her relief a wave of emotion strong enough to make him pause just inside the door.

"Zemanni," she cried. "You're *you* again."

Bron didn't know what that meant. She ran forward and embraced the Scorpiian. He looked surprised, but patted her back awkwardly.

"That's the first time I think anyone's been happy about that," he said.

Bron chuckled as he approached, Olivia's happiness spilling into him. Tethis hovered nearby, looking unhappy.

"We have repaired him to the extent of our technology," she said. "You were correct—his shapeshifting ability is quite limited. It is nothing short of miraculous that he has survived his injuries this long. We have assisted him in resuming the form he requested, but he cannot transform again."

Zemanni scowled at her, but then turned to Olivia and said, "Are we done here?"

"Quite," Tethis said.

Olivia looked at Bron, her eyes filled with hope. He nodded, and she smiled.

"Yes, we're done," she said.

"Fan-freaking-tastic." Zemanni threw his legs over the side of the bed and stood, then fell right back to sitting on it. Olivia rushed forward to steady him.

"Cygnian," Zemanni said. "Help me out here."

The request surprised Bron, but he strode forward. He drew the Scorpiian's arm over his shoulders and helped him to stand.

"Get me out of here," Zemanni murmured.

"Gladly," Bron said.

Olivia reached out and clasped Iridia's hand as they passed. Perhaps someday the Psiarae would be ready to join the other civilizations in this galaxy. When Iridia became their leader, Bron had no doubt she would make strides in that regard. For now, he only wanted to return to his prism and Olivia's homeworld.

Tethis and her personal guard followed them to the hangar bay, though the woman said nothing. They boarded as quickly as they could. Zemanni collapsed in the closest chair once they reached the bridge and didn't even complain when Bron took the command seat before linking up with the ship. He could feel Olivia's tension as they rose through the Psiaraen ocean. Bron shared it. Once they had blasted through the ice and saw stars around them, they all breathed easier. Except perhaps for Zemanni.

The Scorpiian did not look well. Olivia fussed over him while Bron dropped the ship into blue space and set a course that would take them back to the Sol system. Once he was done, he joined her at Zemanni's side.

"I thought Tethis said she healed you," Bron said.

"She did what she could." Zemanni swallowed, his throat obviously working hard to do so. "Being torn apart by a Lyrian leaves a mark. Several marks."

"Being stabbed doesn't help either," Olivia said, her voice colder than Bron had ever heard it. Rage simmered beneath her calm demeanor, her Cygnian soul making itself known with a desire for battle. "I don't think I've ever hated anyone before."

Zemanni shook his head weakly. "He's just doing what he thinks he needs to do."

"After what Dean did to you, how can you defend him?" Olivia said.

"Because I'm supposed to." Zemanni closed his eyes. "I was always supposed to. And I failed."

"Was he on some sort of mission?" she asked. When Zemanni didn't answer, she ran her hand over his forehead. "You're burning up. What is it with you guys? Bron's feverish on the trip here. Zemanni's feverish on the trip back."

"It'll pass," Zemanni said. "Don't worry about it."

"You're my friend—of course I'm worried about it." Her eyes glimmered. Bron stood behind her and placed a hand on her shoulder. Her gratitude flowed through him, along with her desire to comfort her friend. "You got hurt helping me. I'm so sorry this happened to you."

"I'm not." Zemanni said.

Bron searched for something to say to help ease Zemanni's suffering. "There is no shame in losing against a stronger enemy."

Zemanni's eyes snapped open, and he glared up at Bron. "He isn't my enemy."

Bron's spine plates twitched along his back. If Dean was not Zemanni's enemy, did that make them allies? Or was it some sort of misguided Scorpiian loyalty? If so, clearly it wasn't a loyalty that Dean shared.

"Hey, we're just trying to figure things out." Olivia's voice had gentled. She gripped Zemanni's hand and once again wiped his forehead clear. "You called out to him as he was leaving and he stopped. You used a different name. Zakarri?"

Zemanni leaned back and closed his eyes. His mouth

was a grim line and a deep furrow carved its way between his eyebrows.

Olivia shook her head. "What is he to you?" she asked.

Zemanni took a deep breath and let it out slowly. Time stretched on long enough that Bron thought Zemanni wouldn't answer. But then he did.

"He's my brother."

The shock that coursed through Bron echoed back from Olivia. Zemanni and Dean were brothers? Bron thought of his own brother, Dorn, and the complexities of their relationship. Through everything, the bond they shared could never be severed. They had each other's backs. But Dean had tried to kill Zemanni.

"I don't believe this," Olivia said. "Did you know?"

Zemanni shook his head. "Not until he stabbed me. Not until... Not until he tried to bleed me of my quicksilver."

"Zemanni." Olivia clasped his hand and held it. Bron was struck once more at how lucky he was to have a soulmate with such a giving heart. He was grateful that Zemanni had a friend such as her while dealing with this.

"I don't understand what happened," Zemanni said, his gaze becoming unfocused. "Zakarri was always sickly. Scorpiians aren't loving or kind by nature, and our parents are worse than most. All they care about is accomplishment and strategy and position. As long as I was making a name for our family, I thought they would take care of him. But then I returned after a mission and he was gone."

Zemanni turned to Olivia, silver lingering at the edges of his eyes, but not covering his irises. The anguish on his features left no doubt in Bron's hearts that he cared deeply for his brother. Bron never would have believed he could feel kinship with a Scorpiian, but in that moment, he knew it was so.

"They didn't even know where he was," Zemanni said. "When I demanded to be told what had happened to him, when I asked if they had sent him to the vapor pits…" He shuddered and looked away. "They didn't even know. Just that one day, he was home. And then, he wasn't."

"I'm so sorry," Olivia whispered. "But you have to understand that Dean—Zakarri… He has done things. Unforgivable things."

Bron stepped up behind her and rested his hands on her arms. "Not unforgivable. Things that he most atone for."

Zemanni turned to him, his lips parting in surprise. After a moment, he reached up and grasped Bron's arm. Something passed between them, a silent understanding. Bron would not let Zemanni be alone in this after all he had done for them. And for that to be so… Zakarri couldn't be alone, either.

"We will find a way," Bron said.

Zemanni nodded. "I'm working on it. But I need to rest." He let his hand drop away from Bron and closed his eyes.

"Then rest," Bron said. "I'll see us safely home."

Chapter Twenty-Three

Olivia never dreamed she could be so glad to be back on Earth. After all her adventures, sitting outside of Harbor's Ice Cream parlor felt surreal. She wished she could tell her friends about what had happened, but she and Bron were still trying to keep the Psiarae's secrets. It was a little harder now that Bron was openly displaying the cybernetic aspects of his anatomy, but Peri and Cyan had accompanied them back to Earth. The Vegans had been surprisingly good at leading everyone to believe that Bron's anatomy was their people's doing, without ever actually saying it.

Nancy and Lian sat opposite Olivia. Nancy was picking at some sort of non-fat, no-sugar 'treat' in a clear container and Lian was plowing through her third serving of Rigo's specialty—a tres leches ice cream with a cinnamon-strawberry drizzle served in a huge waffle-cone bowl.

"Seriously, where are you putting all that?" Nancy asked, staring at Lian. "You are eating ten times as much as I've ever seen you eat, but you're losing weight. It's so unfair."

"Well, she's eating for two," Olivia said, smiling at her

friend.

"Eating for *alien* two." Lian glanced over at Nancy with glowing red eyes. "This metabolism boost is insane. And have I shown you how tough my skin is now? Let me go get one of Rigo's knives."

She started to rise, but Nancy grabbed her elbow and held on. "No knives, pretty please. You know it freaks me out when you show off that trick."

"I'm stronger now, too," Lian said, grinning as she stared at Nancy's hand on her elbow.

"Come on," Nancy pleaded.

"Fine." Lian sat back down and started eating again.

"Ugh, and I can't believe your eyes have changed to that super cool color," Nancy said. "They're like perfectly matched with Nuar's. It's so romantic and cool." Nancy angled her head, studying their friend. "You need a new wardrobe. Your skin is turning blue, and nothing you own will really make that pop."

Lian grumbled something that sounded suspiciously like, "I'll make you pop."

Nancy rolled her eyes at Lian, then turned her attention to Olivia. "What about you?" Nancy said with a conspiratorial smile. "Are you enjoying the newlywed... newly... bonded life or whatever with Bron?"

"It is absolutely wonderful," Olivia said.

"And what a way to start," Nancy said. "Going on a secret mission to save your soulmate. Ugh, it's all so freaking romantic. I'm totally jealous. Wait, why aren't you eating?"

Olivia pushed her ice cream aside. "My stomach's been a little off since I got back."

"Finally, a downside to your incredibly adventurous lives," Nancy said. "Interstellar travel through blue space. I bet that'll make you motion sick."

Lian shrugged. "I haven't done much of that yet, but it never bothered me. Now, the first week or so with this little girl." She patted her belly, where a slight bump was just starting to show.

"Yeah, but Olivia doesn't have to worry about that." Nancy's eyes widened and her mouth dropped open as Lian let out a scolding tsk.

The sting that Olivia often felt at being reminded of her situation wasn't as sharp as usual. She had Bron to help her face all of life's challenges now. The thought of them not being able to have children weighed on her, but she didn't have to carry that weight alone anymore. It gave her the strength to let herself hope.

"I am so sorry," Nancy said, turning to Olivia. "That was so insensitive of me. I didn't think."

"It's okay," Olivia said. "Bron is... He's enough. We already talked about it. When we're ready, we'll talk to the Vegans to see if they can help us and we'll also look into adoption."

Nancy reached across the table and squeezed Olivia's

hand. "I don't deserve you," Nancy said. "Bron deserves you. Me? Not so much."

"Don't be silly." Olivia patted her hand. "Of course you do. You're my best friend."

Lian cleared her throat. Olivia reached out with her other hand and rested it on top of Lian's.

"You're both my best friends," she said.

"Well then," Nancy said. "Would either of my best friends care to introduce me to that yummy Cygnian pilot, Rom?"

Lian groaned and pulled her hand away, focusing on her ice cream once more. Olivia only laughed.

"Or maybe the mysterious engineer, Tarn?" Nancy waggled her eyebrows.

"Tarn is way too introverted for you," Lian said. "It'd have to be Rom if you're looking for a soulmate in the prism."

"Fine then." Nancy bounced in her seat. "I'm not picky. When can I meet him?"

"We'll see what we can do." Olivia laughed, but paused as a wave of dizziness assailed her. A frisson of pleasure raced along her spine. "Bron and Nuar are back."

A moment later, the men turned a corner and appeared down the street, Bron holding Zorro's lead and Nuar walking Lian's Saint Bernard, Ed. They smiled as they approached the group. Nuar took one look at Lian's nearly empty ice cream waffle cone and simply handed her the leash before he headed straight into the ice cream parlor.

"Well, he's certainly well-trained," Nancy said.

"Eh." Lian shrugged. "We're getting there."

Bron sat next to Olivia. "It's a cool morning," he said. "The dogs enjoyed their walks."

"Thank you for taking him." Olivia leaned in to press a kiss to his lips.

"Oh, come on, get a room," Nancy said, rolling her eyes.

"We have one on the *Arrow*..." He smirked at her, then ran his fingertips lightly down her back. "Are you feeling any better?"

"The fresh air is helping." Olivia shrugged, still fighting off that odd dizziness. Her eyes burned, a headache brewing behind them. Now was not the time to develop migraines.

"We should take you to see the Vegans," Bron said. "It's been three days."

"I know." Olivia shook her head, then looked up at the beautiful summer sky. The idea of being in a hospital, even a Vegan one, was not appealing. "I just—"

Nancy's eyes widened, and she let out a high yelp. She started swatting Lian's shoulder, hard enough that Lian's ice cream went flying from her spoon.

"Hey," Lian yelled. She looked down at Nancy's hand, which was still flailing against her arm. "What the hell is wrong with you?"

Nancy made a series of incoherent noises, tugging on Lian's arm now with both hands, then finally said, "Look!"

Lian turned to Olivia, and her mouth dropped open. Her eyes widened, her red irises glowing brightly as tears quickly flooded over their edges.

"Oh my god, oh my god, oh my god," Lian chanted, swatting at Nancy.

"Ow!" Nancy said. "Cygnian strength."

"Sorry," Lian said, sniffling.

They turned back to Olivia and both of them were crying.

"What is the matter with you two?" Olivia said.

In unison, they pointed at Olivia's face and said, "Bron…" at the same time.

Bron had been staring at them as well, a puzzled expression on his face. He turned to Olivia and his eyebrows hiked up his forehead. His mouth dropped open, his eyes brightening like fires had been lit behind them. He reached out and cupped her face in his hands.

"What is going on?" Olivia demanded.

"Olivia," he said.

A gentle vibration started up in her wristbands, letting her know he had activated them with his cybernetics. No shields rippled over her skin and she couldn't think what else he'd be using them for, except perhaps to scan her. Was something wrong? She could feel Bron's intense focus, his concern and an underlying hope that he was trying desperately to temper.

"You're all freaking me out," she said.

Nancy fumbled in her purse and pulled out her compact. She opened it and held it out to Olivia.

"Look," Nancy said, casting one of her brilliant smiles at Olivia.

Olivia took it and held it up in front of herself, scrutinizing her face. Light glinted off of the mirror, making it hard to see. An oddly blue-tinged light. It took several moments of adjusting the angle she held it at to realize the light was coming from her. From her eyes. Her bright blue eyes—eyes the same color as Bron's.

"I don't..." Olivia began. "This can't... I mean..."

Bron smiled up at her with so much love pouring through their bond, her heart felt as though it would burst from it. He nodded and said, "It's true."

He lifted her free hand, and a hologram flickered into view above its wristband. Olivia recognized her silhouette rotating slowly, her body made up of pale blue lines that preserved her modesty. The image zoomed in on her abdomen, closer and closer until she could see four tiny, pulsing sparks of light.

She didn't dare let herself hope she was seeing what she thought she was seeing. She had to hear it from Bron's lips before she would believe. He grasped her face and pulled her in for a deep, claiming kiss. Her spine lit up with pleasure that coursed over her skin. It was almost enough to distract her. But not really. Bron pulled back, leaving their foreheads touching. The powerful, fast beat of his hearts swept hers away with his.

"What does this mean?" she asked.

He smiled and said, "Twins."

The joy that radiated through her at that word took her breath away. She laughed as tears coursed down her cheeks. This was the beginning of a new world—for her, for Bron, for all of their people. Olivia couldn't wait to explore the bright future before them.

Epilogue

Zakarri rested his head on his palms, his elbows propped against the command console of his severely damaged ship. Once more, he had faced a Cygnian, and once more, he was left empty-handed. He ran his fingers through his hair, turning it into even more of a tousled mess.

Hayley liked that look. She had told him so when she ran her delicate fingers through his hair and smiled at him as if...

As if he mattered.

Zakarri stood and paced in the small space, waiting for the ship's automated systems to repair the damned airlock enough for him to drop into blue space and go... somewhere else. He had no idea where to go next or what to do. He didn't know where Hayley was.

Bron would be on guard now. There wouldn't be another chance to take him. The lockbox was beyond his reach as well. The Cygnians would all be guarding their soulmates more closely than ever, and Zakarri would be alone, as he had always been. Until he'd met her.

He reached into his pocket and pulled out a tattered

photograph. Hayley and himself at her favorite restaurant in Paris. She was looking at the camera with a beautiful smile on her face. Zakarri was staring at her.

She had been a target. A mission. He knew better than to get involved. But they had fit together so perfectly. She hadn't understood when he tried to explain who he was. *What* he was. He never had a chance to convince her they belonged together. All because of Norem.

Zakarri shuddered as he thought of the torment she must be going through. Of the experiments the mad Tau Ceti scientist would conduct on her. Zakarri should never have left her with him. He should never have left her at all.

"I'll never give up," he said. "I will find you." He lightly traced her face with his fingertip. "Even if I have to burn the entire universe to do it."

—

Thank you so much for reading *Bron: A Scifi Alien Warriors Romance*! Bron's book reveals secrets that Zemanni and Zakarri have been holding close for over half a dozen books that span two series! I've been so excited to share their connection with you. And Cygnian-human babies are finally on the way!

The adventures will continue in book six in the *Cygnian 7* series, *Tarn: A Scifi Alien Warriors Romance!* Tarn gave me the most trouble of all the Cygnians, but now that we know each other better, I can't wait to share his story with you! Here is a rather intense peek into the rough draft of his 'meet-cute' with Nancy... (spoiler: it's more like '*heat-cute!*').

Tarn: A Scifi Alien Warriors Romance

Cygnian 7
Book Six

The *Arrow* had become a ghost ship. Kral, Lar, and Dorn had yet to return from helping their soulmates resettle their family in Harbor, Kansas, where they would be safe from targeting by the Cygnian's enemies. Nuar and Bron would stay on Earth indefinitely, raising their families on their soulmates' homeworld—which, conveniently, was under the protection of the most technologically advanced sentients in the galaxy, the Vegans. And Rom was on a date, hopefully meeting his own soulmate.

Every other member of Tarn's prism was back on Earth, leaving him alone on the crystalline vessel. With how little he left engineering, Tarn could understand why they might think he enjoyed solitude, but he actually hated it. And Tarn was certain he was going to be alone much more in the future. He was about to be the last member of their prism to not have a soulmate of his own.

He wanted to be happy for the others. He *was* happy for them. But, until Earth, Tarn had been the only one who spoke of finding a soulmate. He had been the sole member of their prism who held out hope that someday, he would find her. He was desperate to find her. It seemed like he would be the last of the warriors to do so—if he found her at all.

His hearts felt pinched in his chest, their discordant beats driving his irritation higher. Rom was a pilot. He could fly off to meet Earthlings who might be his match, or enjoy the company of women who weren't. A shudder skittered down Tarn's spine. He didn't understand how Rom could share his body with anyone else, knowing that his soulmate was out there.

"Focus on the work," Tarn murmured.

He had other priorities weighing on him. They had been guarding a secret Tau Ceti base that had been built in the asteroid belt between Jupiter and Mars. Norem, the scientist behind the base, had conducted bizarre experiments there. Tarn hadn't even been able to figure out the objective of some of them, even with the help of two Vegans.

The Vegans, Peri and Cyan, were putting all their

attention on studying a trio of Tau Ceti soldiers who had somehow been infused with both human and Cygnian DNA, making them what Cyan called Tau-Cygnian hybrids. Tarn didn't care what Cyan did with her time, and the xenobiologist's interest in studying them made sense. But the soldiers had also been turned into cyborgs, and that meant that Peri, the Vegan engineer, was helping with them as well.

Tarn understood that Alek and Merek needed help adjusting to their new existence, since they had only recently emerged from their transition tanks. But the third cyborg, Tobek, had been functioning fine for a long time and he had been part of the same experiment. The other two were probably not in any immediate danger, and there were things going on in the base that none of them understood. Experiments and technology that might be ticking bombs—literally. Tarn needed Peri's help to decipher them, but Peri's attention was fully on helping Cyan and the cyborgs. How could Tarn do this alone?

Alone... alone... alone...

The word echoed in his mind, taunting him. He slammed his hand down on the console before him. Waves of opalescence flowed out from the site of the impact. No one was even around to feel the vibration of his anger. He pushed away from the station, pacing the length of the engineering bay. Had it always been this small? He felt cramped. Boxed in. Like there was too much near him, even though the bay was spacious.

His skin prickled and his claws extended. He wanted to fight someone, but again, he was alone. There was no one to even talk to. Not that he usually wanted to talk. But there was no one for him to listen to. No one to be close to. It reminded him too much of his childhood in the temple back on Cygnus-Prime.

His mother had always been so busy with her duties as the High Priestess. Tarn was expected to study the texts and join the clergy, but he had more often found himself in mechanical closets or maintenance bays, fine-tuning the technology that made their lives easier. Once again, he was stuck making everything run better with no one to even realize he was there.

Energy coursed down his spine, flowing into his spine plates and making them snap up and vibrate. More flowed through his limbs, over his back and chest. He needed to get out of engineering. He needed to get off the ship. Maybe check in with Peri and the others in the base's cybernetics laboratory. But if Tarn left, the ship would be unmanned. He hated doing that to the *Arrow*.

He ran his hand over his face and sighed. This wasn't helping. He needed to act, needed to move. The ship was enormous, and it was empty. He headed out of engineering, jogging through the corridors to get some of this irritating energy out of his system. His spine plates still wouldn't rest against his back.

He ran faster, weaving through the corridors and jumping up to higher levels. Something was calling to him, some need he couldn't identify. Another mystery for him to unravel. Bron had grown crystal lattices so that the Earthlings among them could climb between decks, but Tarn ignored them. He kept moving. Going up, up, up, till he was at the top of the ship. Where Rom's shard docked.

Rom was back, standing at the far end of the corridor. A large bag rested on the floor a few paces away from him. Tarn had been so wrapped up in his work, he hadn't even realized the shard had returned. More energy pulsed down his spine. His spine plates hummed as they vibrated intensely. His hearts felt as though they might burst any moment, his skin electrified with energy.

Rom was bent over someone, facing away from Tarn. Had he brought the Earthling back with him? That must mean she was his soulmate. But if the woman was Rom's soulmate, why were his spine plates flat against his back? Surely, he wouldn't have brought one of his romantic conquests all the way back to the *Arrow*.

Rom stepped aside, revealing the small Earthling standing next to him. Her hair was the same gold as Earth's sun, her eyes as blue as the summer sky. She had delicate, rounded features and a trim build. Tarn's hearts stuttered, then began pounding frantically. He could barely breathe. His spine plates increased their vibration, resonating through the crystal walls surrounding him strong enough to send rainbows flowing along their surfaces.

She was smiling, and Tarn swore the light of her smile was brighter than the glow from the crystal walls surrounding her. But she was smiling at Rom.

Rom, who stood close to her.

Rom, who had his hands casually resting on her shoulders.

Rom, who was *touching Tarn's soulmate.*

Tarn's mind clouded with rage. He charged down the corridor. The woman's smile vanished, her eyes wide and mouth dropping open as she stared at Tarn. Rom spun around and lunged to the side to meet Tarn's attack, moving their fight away from the woman. Tarn launched himself into the air, pulling back his arm for his strike. He came down with all the force he could gather, slamming his fist into Rom's face. The other Cygnian staggered, the blow almost taking him to his knees.

The woman screamed, but Rom waved her away, laughing. *Laughing.*

How much time had they spent together on Earth? Had Rom seen her as just another conquest?

"Just hang on a minute, Tarn," Rom said.

Tarn struck again, using the heel of his palm against Rom's sternum to force the wind from Rom's lungs. Rom crumpled forward, one hand going to his chest. Pressing his attack, Tarn lunged, grabbing Rom's tunic and using it to lift Rom over his head. Tarn threw Rom as hard as he could. Rom flew down the corridor, hitting the floor and skidding to a stop at the farthest wall.

"Stop," the woman yelled.

But Rom was drawing himself to his feet, his violet eyes glowing with an unmistakable challenge. Tarn let out a low growl, bracing his feet to meet Rom's inevitable attack.

"Oh my god, this is so not how I imagined this happening," the woman said. "You just... shoo!" She waved her hands at Rom.

"Sorry, sweetheart," Rom said. "This fight's not over yet."

"Sweetheart?" Tarn yelled. "Sweetheart?" Just what had happened on their date?

"Please," she said, rolling her eyes. "I've got this."

"You think you can handle a Cygnian warrior who's that fired up?" Rom scoffed.

Tarn stepped between them. Rom was right about this fight not being over. Tarn would pummel him, proving that Tarn was the better warrior. Proving his worth to his soulmate.

He lowered his shoulders to charge Rom again when a sudden burst of ecstasy rushed through Tarn's body, extinguishing his rage. His back arched and his knees buckled. He landed on all fours, his clawed fingertips scraping the floor, etching thin lines of rainbows in the crystal as the pleasure intensified.

The woman—his soulmate—had grabbed him by his spine plates.

Tarn turned to face her, panting with need. Her pale skin was flushed bright pink, and her own breath came in quick gasps. Her pupils were huge with desire, their bond letting her feel the exquisite torture that her touch was inflicting on him.

"I'm gone," Rom said. Tarn barely heard Rom's feet hitting the deck below them over the blood rushing through his ears.

Did she know what she was doing to him? What it meant—what it did—to a Cygnian to be touched in this way? She looked at her hand on his spine plates... and smiled. Satisfaction laced the waves of lust flowing to him through their nascent soul bond. She knew exactly what she was doing. She wanted to affect him this way. Wanted... him.

The Earthling released her grip, and Tarn rose, grabbing her by her waist and drawing her closer. He crushed his lips to hers in a searing kiss. His body was on fire with need for her. She let out a little moan, then wrapped her arms around his neck. Her nails scraped against his skin as she pressed herself to him, each touch conveying a desperation Tarn echoed.

Hope, desire, longing. Tarn didn't know if he was feeling his own emotions or hers. It didn't matter. They were one.

Tarn deepened the kiss, his tongue plunging into her mouth. She moaned again, welcoming him, meeting his thrusts with more a dance than a battle. Her joy flowed out to him, filling his hearts. Their beats drew closer together, matching the quick beat of her own heart. He sensed her need, her desire, through their bond, her happiness flooding every cell in his body.

He reached between them and sliced through the fabric of her pants with his claws, careful not to nick her skin. She gasped as he pulled them away, tossing them down the corridor. His dicks were so hard. He'd never felt anything like it. He ground against her, desperate to be one with her. As quickly as he could, he undid his pants, freeing his erections, then looped a finger through the thin fabric of her panties, tearing them from her with his claws.

He lifted her from her feet and she wrapped her legs around his waist, locking her ankles behind him. Lining up his secondary dick, he placed his crown against her core, barely parting her slick flesh. She wriggled her hips against him, her fingertips pressing against his skin. He had to be careful. He should have given her his wristbands to protect her.

With every ounce of strength he had, he made himself pause, breaking off the kiss and resting his forehead against her shoulder. She let out a little whimpering moan, the sound full of need. Then she reached behind him and grasped his spine plates again.

Tarn threw his head back as every nerve in his body came alive with pleasure. His body arched again, his hips thrusting forward, impaling her on his shaft. Panic fought with pleasure as she cried out, but then he felt a rhythmic pulse deep in her core where they were joined. Instinct took over. He thrust into her, hard and fast, as his own release tore through his body.

She finally released his spine plates, letting him focus on the ecstasy of where they were joined. Without slowing, he pulled his secondary dick from her and buried himself deep with his primary. He couldn't look away from her, watching her face for any sign that he was hurting her. Her eyes were pinched shut, her mouth open to gasp in air. All he sensed from her was pleasure and more of the purest joy he had ever experienced. He gripped her thigh to help support her weight and braced his other arm against the wall, locking his joints into place to make sure he didn't press to close. Then he let himself go.

Each time he sank into her, flames raced along his nerves. She was so tight and wet, her core pulling against him with every stroke. His skin was electrified, every nerve ending on fire. A deep, pulsing pleasure spread out from where they were joined, lighting up his body, filling him with her energy, making them whole. The little noises she made encouraged him, the way she rocked her hips in time with his movements. He landed harder, thrust faster, his heartbeats quickening, until at last in an explosion of sensation, they joined as one.

Still buried deep, he held her against the wall, not knowing what to do next. He had found his soulmate. They had achieved unity. The corridor was lit with rainbows suspended in the air all around them. The woman sagged against him, a contented smile on her face. Tarn was grateful her eyes were closed, so that she couldn't see the confusion that was undoubtedly on his face. It was only a matter of time before she sensed it through their bond.

Nuar had warned them they needed to do certain things to get their Earthling soulmates ready for their union, emotionally and physically. Tarn had blown past all of that. They hadn't even really spoken to each other before bonding. He understood engines and machines, not relationships. But even he realized this was not the way things were supposed to progress. He had joined with this woman, and he didn't even know her name.

Now… what was he supposed to do?

———

Unity is only the beginning of Tarn and Nancy's adventures. There's a lot more in store for them as they unravel the secrets of the Tau Ceti base on Ceres. Be sure to watch for the next *Cygnian 7* book, *Tarn: A Scifi Alien*

Warriors Romance!

If you want to learn more about Bron and the other Cygnian warriors' universe, you can check out *The Department of Homeworld Security* adventures. Many of the novellas have been collected in the first two series omnibuses, *The Department of Homeworld Security Omnibus 1* and *The Department of Homeworld Security Omnibus 2*. Or you can pick and choose with the individual novellas. You'll want to check out *Duration of Stay* to meet the Earthling who won Zemanni's heart and *Nothing to Declare* for the very first appearance of Dean.

I'd love to keep in touch. Join my newsletter at sendfox.com/cassandrachandler to hear about all the adventures happening in Cassland. And if you enjoyed this book, please consider leaving a review at your favorite book review site. I'd really appreciate it—reviews help readers and authors alike!

Thank you for reading *Bron: A Scifi Alien Warriors Romance!*

Cassandra Chandler

About the Author

USA Today Bestselling author Cassandra Chandler uses her vivid imagination to make the world more interesting, spawning the ideas she turns into her captivating Science Fiction Romances and enthralling Paranormal and Urban Fantasy Romances. Fast-paced and funny, lighthearted or filled with suspense, her stories will introduce you to characters you'll fall in love with and worlds you long to explore.